BORISOV

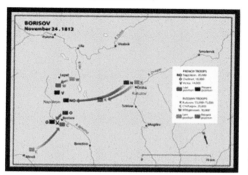

LESNAYA

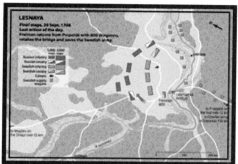

Napoleon, Charles XII, and Hitler

Challenge and Calamity in Russia

STALINGRAD

Af Jochnick

To our friend RICHARD

adolf

PAGE PUBLISHING, INC.
New York, NY

First originally published by Page Publishing, Inc. 2017

ISBN 978-1-63568-972-3 (Paperback)
ISBN 978-1-63568-973-0 (Digital)

Printed in the United States of America

ACKNOWLEDGMENTS

Richard Woodworth, a journalist, a former editor of several newspapers, and author of many successful books has been my editor. He has reviewed and corrected the text and has been indispensable in getting the book designed and formatted for printing.

Alistair Dinwiddie, a well-known mapmaker, has performed excellent work in turning rough and incomplete drawings into readable and attractive maps.

My wife, Liz, has commented on and corrected the text. In addition, as on previous occasions, she has been amazingly successful in locating hard-to-find, badly needed source material. She has shown endless tolerance for the intrusion in ordinary life caused by this project and has provided continuing moral support.

Both of our daughters have been helpful in relation to the front page. Ann came up with a new idea for the design of the initial page. Daphne has created a painting to match the one that she did for my previous book, which will appear as a front page if a second printing becomes desirable. In addition, they offered good suggestions to improve the text.

I have also received valuable comments and ideas concerning the book from our good friends, Tom Jahn and Henning Hamilton.

To all of you who have invested time and efforts to assist me, without which this project could not have been realized, I express my greatest appreciation. Writing a book is an activity that makes you realize the value of help.

CONTENTS

MAPS

INTRODUCTION

In the last three hundred years, Russia has been invaded three times: by Charles XII of Sweden in 1707–09, by Napoleon in 1812, and by Hitler in 1941–45. None of these attempts to conquer Russia succeeded. The three campaigns deserve attention because all were exceptionally important. Had Peter the Great been defeated by Charles, his many significant and progressive reforms of Russian social, political, and religious life and great improvements of its industry and military might have been reversed. Russia's entry as a major force in European political life would have been much delayed. Napoleon was only forty-three when he began the 1812 invasion of Russia. Had his drastic move succeeded, or had he decided to terminate the campaign against Tsar Alexander in time, before losses became excessive, the Napoleonic rule in France and many areas of Europe might have continued for a long time.

It was fairly obvious to observers at the time that the outcome of Hitler's attack on the Soviet Union in 1941 would play a decisive role in the outcome of World War II. Nonetheless, few people would have been able to predict the immediate or long-term effects of a German victory. Would the British have agreed to a negotiated peace (a German victory might have happened before the United States was even in the war), or would they have fought on supported by their Empire and an eventual participation by the United States? And if so, who would eventually have won?

These issues are fascinating, but they are beyond the scope of this study. Instead, it will seek answers to a number of questions more directly involved in the campaigns, such as: Why did the leaders make certain critical decisions? Could the campaigns have ended differently if different decisions had been made? What impact did the size and conditions of the Russian landscape and of the Russian weather have? In addition, a comparison between the three campaigns is justified: the nature of the leaders and their approach to command; how the defending commanders and armies acted; was the purpose the same in all the campaigns, or were there differences; were the campaigns equally affected by the Russian nature and weather, and many other aspects. There were similarities and differences in all areas, deserving further study. This project does not provide a complete account of the three campaigns. Instead, it concentrates on the events that required major strategic and/or tactical decisions. In relation to Germany's June 1941 invasion, for instance, only significant events up to and through the Kursk offensive in July 1943 are covered. There is no account of events beyond that date because those events did not require any significant strategic or tactical decisions.

As a general proposition, a tremendous amount of source material is available in respect to most relevant areas of the campaigns. However, there are exceptions, especially concerning the Soviet military during World War II. The Soviet authorities were quite reluctant to provide significant and reliable information about various aspects of the Soviet military and its performance during that war. The sources upon which this work relies cannot possibly cover all important events of the three campaigns. The sources do, however, offer sufficient information to provide a picture of the events, making possible both an evaluation of the conduct of the principal actors and a comparison between the three campaigns.

The German campaign beginning in 1941 presents some problems, when comparing it with the other two, because the art of war had changed so drastically between the early nineteenth century and the middle of the twentieth. The principal rules for conducting war did not change that much between the times when Charles and Napoleon attempted their earlier invasions. Cavalry was a major force of both armies, and the infantry was used in frontal attacks in 1812 as well as in 1707–09. This study will therefore concentrate initially on Napoleon and Charles. It will start with Napoleon's campaign of 1812. Although that campaign is chronologically second, it was such a major event, involved so many countries, and had such far-reaching consequences that it demands prime attention.

NAPOLEON'S INVASION OF RUSSIA

Background

The French Revolution (1789–1799)

To confront France's mounting financial crisis in 1789, King Louis XVI and his minister of finance called the French National Assembly to meet for the first time since 1616. The assembly consisted of three chambers, one for each estate: the nobility, the clergy, and the common people. The rules of the assembly were such that the nobility and the clergy, although amounting to only 2 percent of France's population, controlled the assembly. The assembly made little progress on the financial situation, but members of the third estate saw the meeting as an opportunity to promote some of the ideas spread by the Enlightenment movement—more rights for the common people and elimination of some of the rules that burdened them. A new National Assembly was created with only one chamber and all members participating on an equal basis. Most of the clergy and some progressive members of the nobility joined this assembly. In June 1789, Louis XVI designated the new National Assembly as the parliament, and all three estates were to belong to it.

An even more dramatic event occurred on July 14, 1789, when masses of artisans and laborers stormed the Bastille in Paris to obtain weapons to fight a potential intervention by the French military, who might take action to protect the king. The early cautious move toward a more democratic system accelerated into a revolution. The Jacobins, the most radical of several competing groups, took control of the National Assembly, which became the National Convention.

The National Convention declared France a republic and arrested the king. In January 1793, he was executed. A reign of terror followed, and many people were accused of counterrevolutionary ideas and killed. Finally, reactions to the terror prompted more moderate groups, led by the Girondists, to replace the Jacobins and their leader, the lawyer Robespierre, who in turn was executed. On August 22, 1795, the National Convention created an executive body, a five-man Directory, to rule the country.

In 1796, the Directory appointed Napoleon Bonaparte commander-in-chief of all troops in Italy in its four-year-old war against Austria. After battling successfully to win French control of Italy, Napoleon returned to Paris in 1799 to find widespread complaints against the Directory for operating in an inefficient and highly corrupt manner. Joseph Sieyès, a key member of the Directory, considered drastic action necessary to improve the situation and avoid a Jacobin return. Together with another member of the five-man group, he planned a coup, but needed the participation of a popular military commander. That position was filled by Napoleon. On November 9, 1799, the conspirators, supported by some other political and military individuals, overthrew the Directory and replaced it with a three-man group, which was named the Consulate. After a stormy session in the General Assembly, Napoleon was approved as First Consul.[1] A few of Napoleon's future marshals, including Bernadotte, opposed both the coup against the Directory and some of the additional steps that solidified Napoleon's power.[2] Following the French victory against the Austrians at Marengo in 1800, Napoleon secured almost unlimited powers. He was made First Consul for life in 1802, and in 1804, he proclaimed himself emperor of France.

The French Revolution had become the central cause for actions and developments in Europe from its start in 1789 until the end of the Napoleonic period in 1815. In 1792, France had declared war against Austria and Prussia because it suspected the two countries of assisting French royalists in staging counterrevolutionary activities. The first coalition against France was created by Britain, Austria, and Italy in 1794 to prevent the new French radical ideas from spreading. Following a peace treaty at Amiens in 1802, Britain again declared war against France in 1803, feeling that the increasing French influence and control over Europe were threatening commercial and political interests critical to Britain. The British-French war continued uninterrupted until 1815, with other European countries, including Austria, Prussia, Russia, Sweden, and Holland, intervening from time to time—usually allied in coalitions with Britain, but sometimes supporting the French.

Emperor Napoleon Bonaparte

Napoleon Bonaparte was born in 1769 in Corsica, the son of Carlo Bonaparte, a successful lawyer. Carlo sent Napoleon and his older brother, Joseph, to a military school in France in 1779. Napoleon went on to a military academy, from which he graduated as a second lieutenant in the artillery in 1786. He returned to Corsica and got involved in the efforts to make Corsica independent from France. Conflicts with the leader of this movement forced Napoleon and the entire Bonaparte family to relocate to France. His military career accelerated in 1795 when the troops that he commanded saved the governing five-man Directorate in Paris from counterrevolutionaries. He was appointed commander-in-chief of the French Army in Italy and married Josephine, the widow of a guillotined general, in 1796. In 1799, he took advantage of an exceptional opportunity, which offered him a path to almost complete power in France as first consul in the Consulate. The disastrous 1812 campaign eventually forced his abdication in 1813. In 1814, he regained his position as emperor, but following his defeat at Waterloo, he was exiled to the island of St. Helena in the South Atlantic, where he died in 1821.

Napoleon as Commander and Administrator

According to most observers, Napoleon's principal talent as a military commander was his ability to implement existing tactics and strategies rather than developing new ones. Fast reaction to changing situations and the ability to move his forces quickly were characteristic of the way he conducted military operations. These traits enabled him to surprise enemies and exploit their weaknesses.

Napoleon reformed and improved the French military. His most significant initiative may have been the creation of the Army Corps. These units included several divisions (traditionally the biggest operating unit) of infantry and cavalry in addition to forty to fifty artillery pieces for a total of twenty thousand or more men. The Army Corps was usually commanded by one of Napoleon's marshals. They were big enough to operate independently of the main Army and provided the French Army increased flexibility for speedy action and surprise. Napoleon placed great emphasis on the morale of his army. In the early years, he shared many of his soldiers' difficulties and conditions. Like Charles XII, he would frequently lead attacks that exposed him to exceptional dangers. Napoleon made sure that those who performed well were recognized and rewarded regardless of rank. This was something French soldiers had not experienced in the past, and it gained him great loyalty, even devotion.

In addition to improvements in the military, Napoleon contributed greatly to the administration of France. The ambitious steps he implemented in the legal realm resulted in the Napoleonic Code that codified the laws of France. It came to form the basis for the civil codes employed by most European nations today. Under his reign,

France was well administered, but he had little tolerance for freedom of speech. Napoleon is credited with an exceptional intellectual capacity, memory, ability to concentrate, and enormous stamina for work. He maintained his strength in all these areas from the start of his command of the French Army in Italy in 1796 at least through his series of victories beginning in 1806 with the remarkable French victory against a combined Austrian-Russian Army at Austerlitz.

This success was followed in 1807 by three more victories; at Jena-Auerstädt against Prussia; at Friedland, where the Russian Army was crushed and Tsar Alexander was persuaded to accept the peace treaty at Tilsit; and finally at Wagram, where Napoleon defeated Archduke Charles of Austria. Many historians have considered the Wagram victory the high mark of the French Empire. All major continental powers had been defeated and agreed to join Napoleon's battle against Britain. About this time, however, Napoleon's energy appeared to have started to lag. His standard eighteen-hour workday had begun affecting his health.[3] A number of historians have suggested that by 1812, Napoleon had declined significantly from the superior standard he had so long maintained as both the executing commander and the intellect behind military moves. His Russian campaign of 1812 provides substantial evidence to support these conclusions. During this later period of his remarkable career, he also became more stubborn and less inclined to listen to the advice of his commanders.

Napoleon's Commanders

The French Revolution gave young men outside the aristocracy the opportunity for military careers. In 1804, Napoleon appointed eighteen senior officers Marshals of the Empire. They belonged to the new group of commanders emerging following the Revolution. They were young, ambitious, brave, generally capable, and often difficult to control. Many came from modest backgrounds. All were fervent supporters of the revolutionary ideas, ruthlessly enforced by the Jacobins and other leaders in Paris. Quite a few had spent time in jail, sometimes suspected of lack of fidelity to the Revolution and sometimes, following Robespierre's fall, for showing excessive zeal in support of the disgraced leader. They were usually given command of a corps, the new Army operating unit that Napoleon had created. In addition to these career officers, Napoleon's commanders included members of his family, among them his brother Jerome and his adopted son Eugene. Marshal Joachim Murat was a special case. He came from a family not related to the Bonapartes, but he married Napoleon's sister and seemed to have received special treatment and rewards. Despite their revolutionary backgrounds and sympathies, these young marshals, like Napoleon himself, appear to have quickly developed an appetite for nobility, even royal positions and titles.[4]

A few historians have questioned the capability of some of these key French commanders. Because of the size of Napoleon's forces and his tactics of quick, unexpected moves, the corps frequently operated with substantial independence. Success for the Army as a whole required a high level of performance by the corps commanders. Napoleon put together the operating plans, but it was critical that a corps, which he had determined to play a certain role, appear at the place and at the time intended. With the rather primitive tools of communications available in the early nineteenth century, this was obviously a challenge.

> **Marshal Joachim Murat**
>
> Joachim Murat was born in 1767 to Pierre Murat, a farmer and innkeeper. Joachim became a loyal supporter of Napoleon in 1795 when he succeeded in getting some artillery pieces into Paris, which helped Napoleon save the National Assembly from counterrevolutionaries. He was a flamboyant, vain, and usually successful cavalry commander and played a key part in critical battles. In 1808, Napoleon, made him king of Naples. The Italian Bourbon branch conquered Naples following Waterloo. Murat lost his life in a failed attempt to recover his crown in 1815.

Nonetheless, Napoleon's commanders usually performed well. At Auerstädt in 1807, Marshal Davout's corps of twenty-eight thousand won an astounding victory against a Prussian force exceeding sixty thousand. At Eylau a few months later, Marshal Murat led literally the entire French cavalry in an unprecedented, dangerous but successful charge against the advancing Russian infantry, which saved Napoleon from a threatened defeat. In early November 1812, with the main Russian force in close pursuit, Napoleon counted Marshal Ney and his rearguard as lost, but Ney reappeared after crossing the frozen Dnieper River with nine hundred survivors[5]. However, the independent attitude of some of the marshals, and their tendency occasionally to indulge in their own preferences or prejudices, could create problems. At Auerstädt in 1807, Marshal Bernadotte was stationed with his corps within operating distance of Marshal Davout's desperate struggle with the Prussians, but despite orders from Napoleon and pleas from Davout, he failed to move in support of Davout. Following Davout's victory, Bernadotte was severely chastised by Napoleon and almost lost his command.[6]

Reasons for War with Russia

In the 1807 Tilsit peace treaty, Tsar Alexander had reluctantly agreed to join Napoleon's battle against the British, including enforcing the Continental System under which no trade with Britain was permitted.[7] However, Alexander gradually concluded that this prohibition imposed an unacceptable cost on the Russian economy. So in 1810 he resumed trade with Britain. All Napoleon's efforts to convince Alexander to remain loyal failed. In addition, there were other causes for friction between the two supposedly allied nations. Influential voices within Napoleon's administration tried to dissuade him from military action against Russia. One of his closest advisors, General Armand de Caulaincourt, French ambassador to Russia from 1807 to 1811, warned him against attacking Russia and told Napoleon he would never be able to impose his terms on Tsar Alexander.[8]

Nonetheless, Napoleon decided that drastic action was necessary, both to stop the leakage in his blockade and to discourage countries like Prussia and Austria from following Russia's lead. So in 1811, Napoleon began to plan a campaign against Russia. The purpose was not to take Russian land or replace Alexander. It was to make Alexander comply with his Tilsit commitment and also to demonstrate to Alexander, as well as to the Austrian and Prussian rulers, that France was the dominant power in Europe.

Tsar Alexander

Alexander was born in 1777 and was crowned tsar in 1801, following the murder of his father, Tsar Paul I, by members of the aristocracy. Alexander is thought to have known of the conspiracy against his father, but the culprits were never punished. In the early part of his reign, he favored idealistic ideas of general, and possibly permanent, peace through international agreements. He is thought to have been easily swayed by changing circumstances and moved back and forth between pro-Napoleon, neutral, and anti-Napoleon positions. During Napoleon's invasion in 1812, he entered an alliance with Sweden, negotiated by Bernadotte, and assisted Sweden in gaining Norway. Despite early reverses in the war of 1812, Alexander rejected all Napoleon's offer of negotiations. He played a significant part in the Congress of Vienna in 1814–15 and in his later years became quite influenced by Prince Metternich, the Austrian foreign minister.

Napoleon's 1812 Campaign

Preparations and Plans

During his successful campaigns in 1806 to 1810, Napoleon and his marshals had defeated Prussia, Austria, and Russia and converted them from enemies to allies in the continuing war against Britain. When Russia defected in 1810, Napoleon was in a position to gain active support from Austria and Prussia and some smaller satellite countries, like Westphalia, governed by Jerome Bonaparte. All these countries provided not only moral support but also troops for the coming battle. Napoleon was able to assemble a force far larger than any previously employed in European wars. Estimates vary, but including all supporting and reserve units, even a conservative calculation would be five hundred thousand to six hundred thousand men. Of this army, no more than 50 to 55 percent were French.

One might wonder why Napoleon felt it necessary—or even desirable—to put together such an enormous force, since he should have known that the Russians had fewer than two hundred thousand troops initially available to oppose his advance. Of these, the First Western Army, commanded by Barclay de Tolly, counted around 120,000. It was stationed in the neighborhood of Vilna, about forty kilometers from the Polish border. The Second Western Army, with General Peter Bagration in command, consisted of about 45,000 men and was located farther south, east of Grodno and north of the Pripet Marshes. A third army of about thirty-five thousand, under General Alexander Tormasov, was stationed at Lutsk, south of the Pripet Marshes. Finally, there was the Moldau Army of thirty-five thousand, commanded by Admiral Pavel Chichagov, which, at the beginning of Napoleon's campaign, was assigned to defend the Ottoman border.

Possibly the emperor hoped that his demonstration of strength would convince Tsar Alexander to come around without a fight and comply with his demands. If those were Napoleon's expectations, he was quickly disappointed. Alexander, far from yielding to Napoleon, initially even contemplated a counterattack against Warsaw. However, before Barclay de Tolly had taken any steps to start this action, he discovered the size of the French Army and promptly amended his plans.

Napoleon's First Goal: Barclay de Tolly

Napoleon crossed the Niemen River near Kovno on June 24 and led his main forces into Russia.[9] He had expected the Russians to put up a major fight close to the border and to have his campaign successfully completed in three weeks. This would have been possible if Barclay de Tolly had been foolish enough to allow his troops to engage in such a battle. But he was not. As soon as he learned that the French Army was crossing the Niemen, Barclay started withdrawing his First Western Army toward the fortressed town of Drissa on the Dvina River, some three hundred kilometers northeast of Vilna.

In his many successful operations in Central Europe, Napoleon had frequently surprised his enemies with quick moves, where confiscated local supplies sustained his troops.

> **Field Marshal Barclay de Tolly**
>
> Barclay de Tolly, a member of the Scottish clan Barclay, was born in 1761 in Livonia, then part of Russia. He began active service in the Imperial Russian Army at age fifteen and subsequently participated in numerous wars against the Ottoman Empire, France, and Sweden. He was commander of the Russian Army that invaded Finland in 1808. Barclay decided that war by moving his army across the frozen Baltic from Vasa to Umea. During Napoleon's invasion in 1812, Barclay commanded Russia's largest army. His continuous retreat originally was strongly criticized by the Russian nobility, and Barclay was replaced by Field Marshal Mikhail Kutuzov. However, following the eventual defeat of Napoleon, Barclay's retreat strategy was reevaluated. Barclay received much praise and many honors from the Tsar and was restored to top command of the Russian forces. He captured Paris in 1815.

This approach was far more difficult in Russia where distances were great, roads were poor, and the products from the local farming community inadequate to provide anything near what his huge force required. Napoleon had arranged for substantial supplies at various depots, but his transportation facilities were inadequate. It quickly became clear that nowhere near enough supplies for the troops and their animals could be provided. In addition, at the start of the campaign in late June, the heat was oppressive. The French Army's advance to Vilna, only forty kilometers beyond the Niemen River, caused the loss of twenty thousand horses. When his forces arrived at Vilna, Napoleon found no Russian Army ready for battle. Instead, the town had been abandoned and all supplies destroyed or removed.

The composition of the two opposing armies and troop movements during the initial period, June 24 to July 10, 1812, were as indicated on the map below (the initials after the names are shown on the map to indicate the moves of the different units):

French Grand Army

Northern Frontier (Riga)
Tenth Corps; MacDonald, M.
    D., 30,000, Prussian
Napoleon, Close Control
Imperial Guard; Mortier, M. O., 47,000
First Corps; Davout, D., 72,000
Second Corps; Oudinot, O., 37,000
Third Corps; Ney, N., 39,000
Three Cavalry Corps; Murat, M., 32,000
Fourth Corps; Eugene, E., 45,000, Italian
Fifth Corps; St. Cyr, S. C., 25,000
The Group of Jerome Bonaparte, J.
Fifth Corps; Poniatowski, P., 36,000, Polish
Eighth Corps; Vandamme, V.,
    17,000, Westphalian
Southern Frontier
Austrian Corps; Schwarzenberg, S., 34,000
Seventh Corps; Renier, R., 17,000, Saxons
Cavalry Corps; L. Maubourg,
    L. M., 8,000, Saxons
Reserve; Ninth Corps. Victor, V., 45,000
Eleventh Corps; Augereau, A., 80,000

The commanders above were senior French officers except MacDonald, a Prussian general; Eugene, Napoleon's adopted son, originally the son of Josephine's first husband; Jerome Bonaparte, Napoleon's brother; Poniatowski, a member of the Polish royal family and the commander of a Polish Army in exile, existing under Napoleon's protection; and Schwarzenberg, an Austrian general.

Russian

First Western Army; Barclay de
    Tolly, B. T., 100,000,
following W. Wittgenstein's 20,000, separation.
Second Western Army, Bagration, B, 45,000
Third Western Army;, Tormasow, T., 35,000
Army of the Moldau; Chichagov, C., 35,000

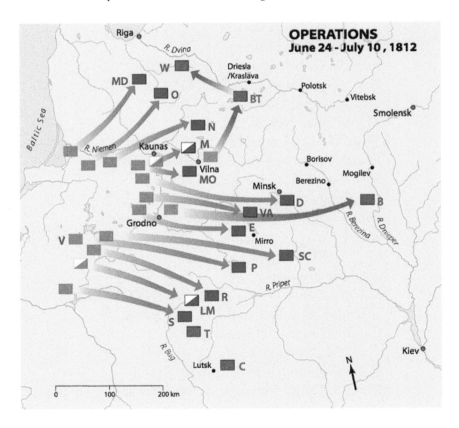

Bagration

Simultaneously with his attempts to engage Barclay's First Western Army, Napoleon had ordered Marshal Davout and his First Corps of seventy-two thousand men—considered by some the best corps in the Army—to move toward Minsk. At the same time, Napoleon's brother, Jerome Bonaparte, was to move his force of seventy-five thousand east from Grodno on the Polish border toward an area south of Davout's corps. The idea was to catch Bagration and his Second Western Army in between Jerome's forces advancing from the west, Davout's troops coming from the north, and the Pripet Marshes in the south. However, the French troops, especially those of Jerome, were too slow. As a result, Bagration, who recognized the danger, moved his army fast enough toward the Berezina River, east of Minsk, to avoid the French maneuver. When Jerome reported this failure to his brother, Napoleon became furious. He removed Jerome from command and assigned his troops to Davout.

Vitebsk and Mogilev

On arriving at the fortress town of Drissa on the Dvina River, Barclay de Tolly quickly realized that this was no place to stage a major defense. The fortress was considered of great importance by the Tsar, who had retained a Prussian general to design it. However, the fortress was badly designed and in a location difficult to defend. So Barclay moved his force farther east along the Dvina to Vitebsk, where he planned to make a stand. Though not really his preferred choice of action, he was under increasing pressure from the Tsar, who was in turn pressured by the nobility in St Petersburg. They felt the Russian Army should not simply retreat, allowing the French to move easily far into Russia. Instead, they felt Barclay should confront the enemy and stop his advance.

Though born in Russia, Barclay de Tolly was of Scottish heritage and many distrusted him as a foreigner and wanted him replaced. His continuous retreat discouraged even some of the Army's officers and soldiers. Responding to this pressure, Barclay decided to launch a counterattack at Vitebsk against the advancing French forces, which were led by Napoleon himself. Approaching Vitebsk from the west, the French noticed large Russian formations in defensive positions ready to block their advance. Napoleon thought he had finally got his chance for a decisive battle. His forces moved up, and on July 26 were in a position to attack. However, Napoleon hesitated. He wanted more of his army to arrive before making the move.

Marshal Louis Davout

Louis Davout, born in 1770, joined the military in 1785. His promising military career was interrupted in 1797 because of suspicions of noble birth. Napoleon brought him back into the military and, recognizing his exceptional military talent, included him among the commanders appointed Marshals of the Empire in 1804. In command of a corps, Davout proceeded to win the astounding victory at Auerstädt against a much superior Prussian force and continued to perform as one of Napoleon's best commanders. Following Napoleon's abdication in 1814, Davout retired, rather than serve the Bourbon government. On his return from Elba, Napoleon appointed Davout Secretary of War. Davout again retired after Napoleon's Waterloo defeat. Although not particularly friendly with Marshal Ney, Davout tried hard to prevent Ney's execution by the Bourbon government. Davout's name appears on the Arc de Triomphe in Paris.

Some observers have speculated that in Napoleon's younger days, he would have attacked immediately. Quick action would have made a difference. Barclay had planned to launch his own counterattack the next day. However, that very night, he received information that Davout's forces had defeated Bagration on July 23 at Mogilev on the Dnieper River. Barclay concluded that this would prevent Bagration from joining him in Vitebsk and perhaps give the French an opportunity to separate Bagration's army from his own. So Barclay changed his plans. He left enough troops to delay the French and immediately withdrew his main force toward Smolensk, about 130 kilometers farther east on the Dnieper. As a result, when Napoleon attacked the next day, he again found that the enemy was gone.

The Mogilev battle on July 23, 1812, was the first major one in the Russian Campaign. Davout's First Corps had taken the town, and since it was an important crossing point on the Dnieper, Bagration tried to take it back. Davout stopped Bagration's attack and made his forces retreat. Nonetheless, this victory only meant some delay in Bagration's move to Smolensk, and its timing proved beneficial to the Russians. It resulted in Barclay avoiding a confrontation, which could have proved disastrous for his army. So Napoleon's frustrations with his Russian invasion continued, and his troops kept suffering from insufficient supplies and the deaths of their horses. The Army's strength was melting away as no reinforcement was possible.

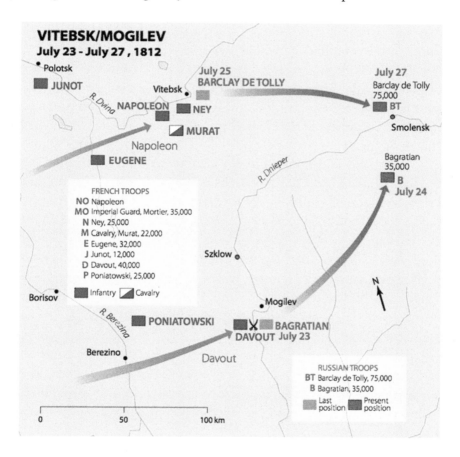

Smolensk

Barclay de Tolly and Bagration both moved their forces toward Smolensk, and on August 4 they joined up somewhat north of the city. Smolensk straddled the Dnieper with the old city, including an old fortress, on the south side and a more modern part north of the river.

After his failure to get the Russian First Western Army engaged in a major battle, Napoleon entered Vitebsk on July 27. He remained there for two weeks. General de Caulaincourt felt that Napoleon fluctuated between deep concern over his heavy losses and modest accomplishment and sudden optimism resulting from positive information of little significance. One day, Napoleon would announce that the campaign would be terminated to avoid failure for lack of supplies; the next day, he would be ready to continue the advance. According to Caulaincourt, he, along with Marshal Berthier, Napoleon's chief of staff, and most of his other senior commanders, tried to convince Napoleon that the campaign could not succeed and should be stopped, but that Napoleon could not be shaken out of his "illusions."[10]

So in the end, Napoleon decided to continue pursuing the Russian Army deeper into Russia. He ordered Marshal Davout and Prince Poniatowski to bring their forces of about 65,000 men along the Dnieper to the town of Orsa, where the river starts flowing south rather than west. With Barclay's and Bagration's forces north and northwest of Smolensk, Napoleon designed a move to cut the enemy's retreat route. The French forces would cross the Dnieper at Orsa, with his own force of around 120,000 crossing slightly east of the town. Then the French Army would proceed past the city of Smolensk advancing south of the river. The leading troops would re-cross the river east of Smolensk and intersect the main route to Moscow. If this maneuver was implemented quickly enough, the Russian Army would find its escape to Moscow cut and would have had to engage in a major battle. Some observers have considered this a potential masterstroke.[11]

The plan held out great promise, especially since Barclay, under pressure from the Tsar, was starting a hesitant advance in a north-westerly direction from Smolensk, intending to attack the French left flank. The advancing Russian troops consisted of an infantry force of about one hundred thousand and twenty thousand cavalry. Barclay's action started on August 7 and continued with stops and starts until

August 14. However, shielded by cavalry, Napoleon had successfully moved his forces south, past the area that Barclay planned to attack. Napoleon had begun to implement his own plan to intersect the road to Moscow, Barclay's retreat route.

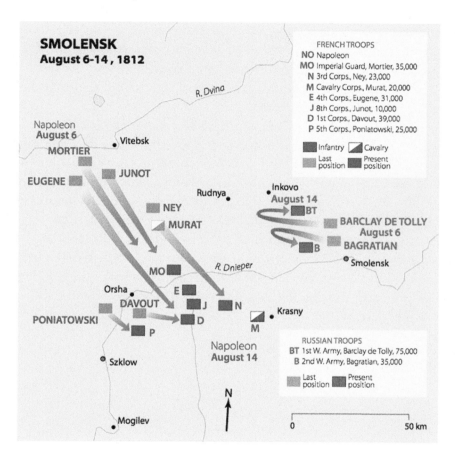

On August 14, Napoleon carried out the first stage of his plan as 175,000 troops had crossed the Dnieper by the end of the day. Murat and Ney led the advance east. In the little suburb of Krasnoi, the French were blocked by a single Russian division. This division repulsed repeated attacks by Murat's cavalry. Murat's failure to coordinate his actions with Ney prevented Ney's infantry from engaging the Russians and delayed the French advance by one critical day. It was important because Barclay had stationed the Russian division south of the Dnieper to guard his left flank while he launched his counterattack against the French northwest of Smolensk. The commander of the Russian troops at Krasnoi reported to Barclay the advance of French troops south of the river. Barclay and Bagration had already started worrying about the location of the French forces and Napoleon's intentions. With the information from Krasnoi, the Russian advance northwest of Smolensk was reversed, and the Russian Army promptly returned to Smolensk and its northern suburbs from the north. The weak defenses of the city, in particular the old fortress, were strengthened.

Then Napoleon seemed to have lost sight of his objectives. Instead of pushing his forces forward as rapidly as possible, he took a day off to review the troops and celebrate his forty-third birthday. Making matters worse, Napoleon then launched frontal attacks against the old Smolensk fortress. The French suffered substantial losses before conquering the fortress, and in the meantime, the encircling movement south of the city was delayed.[12] Upon entering Smolensk, the French found the city abandoned. Barclay had taken advantage of the additional time that Napoleon's distractions had provided, moving his main force out of the city onto the route toward Moscow.

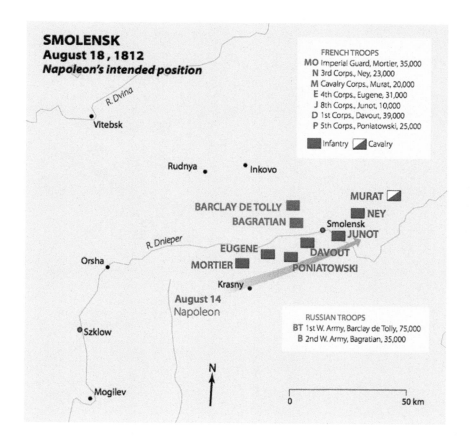

SMOLENSK
August 18, 1812
Napoleon's intended position

FRENCH TROOPS
MO Imperial Guard, Mortier, 35,000
N 3rd Corps., Ney, 23,000
M Cavalry Corps., Murat, 20,000
E 4th Corps., Eugene, 31,000
J 8th Corps., Junot, 10,000
D 1st Corps., Davout, 39,000
P 5th Corps., Poniatowski, 25,000

Infantry   Cavalry

R. Dvina

Vitebsk

Rudnya   Inkovo

MURAT

BARCLAY DE TOLLY   NEY
BAGRATIAN   Smolensk JUNOT
R. Dnieper
EUGENE   DAVOUT
Orsha   MORTIER   PONIATOWSKI
Krasny

August 14
Napoleon

Szklow

RUSSIAN TROOPS
BT 1st W. Army, Barclay de Tolly, 75,000
B 2nd W. Army, Bagratian, 35,000

N

Mogilev

0   50 km

Napoleon made a last attempt to block the retreat of at least part of the Russian Army. Marshal Junot's corps was to play a major part along with troops from Ney and Murat's corps. However, Junot, advancing on the south side of the Dnieper, refused to cross the river at the critical time. Thus, the Russian forces were able to escape, and Napoleon's masterful plan failed as a result of poor execution. As at Vitebsk, he was denied a chance for a decisive battle.

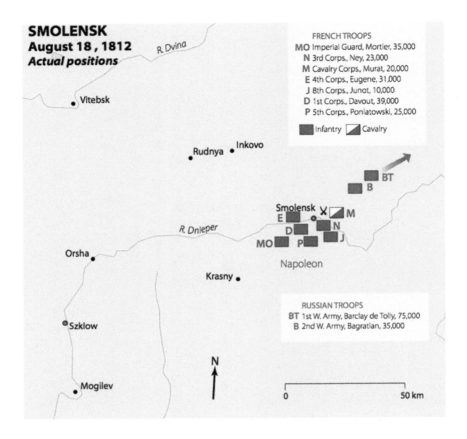

SMOLENSK
August 18, 1812
Actual positions

FRENCH TROOPS
MO Imperial Guard, Mortier, 35,000
N 3rd Corps., Ney, 23,000
M Cavalry Corps., Murat, 20,000
E 4th Corps., Eugene, 31,000
J 8th Corps., Junot, 10,000
D 1st Corps., Davout, 39,000
P 5th Corps., Poniatowski, 25,000

RUSSIAN TROOPS
BT 1st W. Army, Barclay de Tolly, 75,000
B 2nd W. Army, Bagratian, 35,000

Borodino

With the Russian Army retreating toward Moscow on August 20, Tsar Alexander responded to the Russian nobility's pressure and replaced Barclay de Tolly as supreme commander with the old Field Marshal Mikhail Kutuzov. Kutuzov's army career had been long and distinguished. However, he had had the misfortune of commanding the Russian troops in their defeat at Austerlitz and, while mostly not his fault, had been blamed by the Tsar for the loss. Nevertheless, the growing objections to Barclay's strategy of retreat prompted the Tsar to put Kutozov back in command, with instructions to take a stand against Napoleon before he got to Moscow.[13]

Following his latest failure to force the Russian Army into a decisive battle, Napoleon hesitated as he had at Vitebsk. He considered spending the winter in Smolensk to reinforce his army and its supplies. In the end, however, he decided to continue. On August 24, Napoleon resumed his advance toward Moscow.

This decision must have been difficult for Napoleon. He had already brought his army much farther into Russia than he had planned, and he lacked many of the tools needed for such an extended campaign. The biggest problem was obtaining supplies for the troops and animals. There was no way supply from the depots close to Kovno and other towns near the Niemen River could be brought forward fast enough to supply the advancing French Army.

It was hardly surprising that Napoleon's Army had suffered badly during its five-hundred-kilometer advance from Kovno to Vitebsk and on to Smolensk. However, when he saw an opportunity, Napoleon felt he had to move fast in order to catch the Russian Army and force a decisive battle. So he simply accepted the enormous losses in manpower and horses. In his campaign against Peter the Great in 1707–09, Charles XII had experienced the same difficulties in keeping his army supplied. In both cases, the Russian forces' ruthless scorched-earth tactics contributed greatly to the supply problems.

Napoleon had failed in his repeated attempts to make Tsar Alexander negotiate. Still he retained the hope that Alexander would come around as soon as his troops had been decisively defeated. That may have been wishful thinking. Over the previous two months, the relative strength of the French and Russian armies had changed from a three-to-one advantage for the French to less than one and one-half to one at Smolensk. At Borodino, three weeks after the Smolensk confrontations and 250 kilometers farther east, the manpower relationship was almost even, primarily due to the continuing losses incurred by the French. The invaders' steady decline in strength may well have affected Alexander's willingness to negotiate. Napoleon seemed to have assumed that Moscow was so critical a target that if he conquered the former Russian capital, Alexander would feel compelled to negotiate. This assumption was wrong.

About the time in late August when Napoleon led the main French Army out of Smolensk, Alexander was meeting with Napoleon's former marshal, Jean-Baptiste Bernadotte, now the crown prince of

Sweden, on the island of Aland in the Baltic. The two were negotiating terms for Sweden's assistance to Russia in return for Alexander helping Sweden to take Norway from the Danes.

On September 5, the advance French troops reached the small town of Borodino. That was the place that Kutuzov, complying with Alexander's edict, had selected for a major battle. The Kalatsha River, a tributary of the Moscow River, flows southwesterly crossing the two major routes to Moscow, first the new post road and then, three kilometers down the river, the old post road. In between these two routes, the Russian Army had created defenses—mainly quickly dug redoubts. One great redoubt just south of the new post road and three smaller ones, closer to the old one, were referred to as Bagration's fletches. Kutuzov, according to some historians, saw the new post road as a major weakness, offering Napoleon an opportunity to break through and proceed toward Moscow. So he directed Barclay, still commanding the First Western Army, about seventy-five thousand strong, to defend this area along with ten thousand Cossacks commanded by General Matvei Platov. They took positions mostly north of the new post road. Kutuzov also allocated most of the Russian artillery—about four hundred cannons—to this area. The section south of the great redoubt and including the fletches was to be defended by Bagration's force of about thirty-five thousand men, supported by a newly arrived militia force of ten thousand.

Napoleon and his commanders realized that the positions of the Russian forces created an advantage for an attack south of the new post road against Bagration's fletches. Marshal Davout argued for an encircling move farther south to attack the rear of Bagration's army. This might have held great promise and would have been in line with Napoleon's approach in the past—at Austerlitz, for instance. Napoleon, however, was reluctant and apparently felt such a move might let Kutuzov slip away.

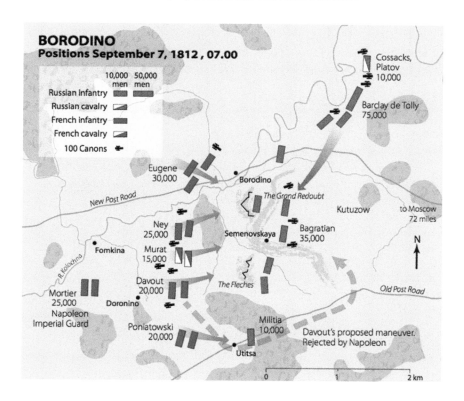

So Napoleon opted for a frontal attack by Marshals Davout and Ney against Bagration's fletches and by Prince Eugene's force against the great redoubt. The fighting for this limited area started early in the morning of September 7, went on until late afternoon, and resulted in tremendous casualties on both sides. Eventually, the French got control of the contested sites, to a significant extent because of Kutusov's faulty troop and artillery allocations. While the French artillery was extremely effective, much of the Russian artillery, stationed too far north, did not come into play.[14]

Late in the afternoon, Ney and Davout urged Napoleon to employ the Imperial Guard, an elite force of twenty thousand held in reserve. Some observers feel that might have given the French a decisive victory. The troops on both sides were exhausted, and Kutuzov had no more reserves to throw in. But Napoleon felt it was too dangerous to risk this one remaining fresh force so far from France.

Kutuzov, having suffered greater losses than the French (thirty-five thousand to forty thousand as compared to twenty-five thousand to thirty thousand), carried out an orderly retreat. In terms of troops involved as well as losses incurred, Borodino was Napoleon's biggest battle so far. How much difference would it have made if Napoleon had won a total victory instead of a fairly modest gain? Perhaps not very much. Napoleon by that time had advanced so far into Russia and suffered such great losses (more than two-thirds of his army) that even a decisive victory at Borodino could hardly have helped him reach the objectives of his Russian campaign or extricated him from the pending disaster.

Marshal Michael Ney

Michael Ney, born in 1769, the son of a barrel-cooper in Lorraine, joined the Army as a noncommissioned officer. Following the revolution, he attained officer's status and at twenty-nine had advanced to general, commanding a brigade. He fought in almost all the big battles from 1796 to 1813 and served Napoleon until the Marshals' Revolt in 1813, when, speaking for the marshals, he demanded Napoleon's abdication. He swore loyalty to the Bourbon monarchy, but following Napoleon's return from Elba, he rejoined Napoleon and commanded the left wing at Waterloo. After Napoleon's defeat, he was convicted of treason by the Bourbon regime and was executed in 1815. However, he was granted the privilege of giving his executioners the order to fire. Despite the conviction, his name is inscribed on the Arc de Triomphe.

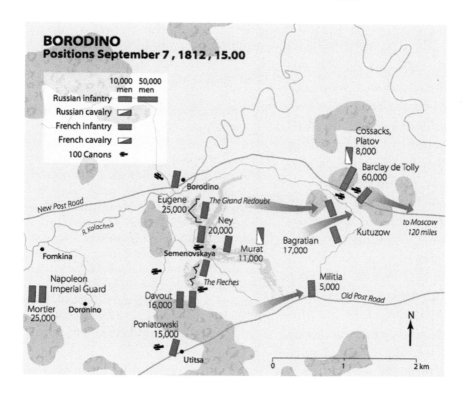

BORODINO
Positions September 7, 1812, 15.00

Russian infantry
Russian cavalry
French infantry
French cavalry
100 Canons

10,000 men / 50,000 men

Cossacks, Platov 8,000
Barclay de Tolly 60,000

Borodino

New Post Road

R. Kolochna

Eugene 25,000
The Grand Redoubt
Ney 20,000
Bagratian 17,000
Murat 11,000
Kutuzow
to Moscow 120 miles

Fomkina
Semenovskaya

Napoleon
Imperial Guard
The Fleches
Militia 5,000
Old Post Road

Mortier 25,000
Doronino
Davout 16,000

Poniatowski 15,000

Utitsa

N

0   1   2 km

Moscow

Following Borodino, Kutuzov faced the question whether Moscow should be defended or simply abandoned to the French. His senior commanders were reportedly split almost fifty-fifty on the issue. Alexander had earlier decided that the city should be defended. However, he changed his mind after receiving Kutuzov's report, which described Borodino as a Russian victory, but also indicated that the Army now needed rest and reinforcements. The Tsar concluded that, at least for the moment, Moscow could be sacrificed. Napoleon had expected that a Russian delegation, seeking peace, would meet him on his entry into Moscow on September 14. No such thing happened. Instead, at the direction of its mayor, Moscow was set on fire, and 75 percent of the city was destroyed. Napoleon had to abandon the Kremlin in favor of a palace outside the city, where he stayed for almost a month. Looking at things with hindsight, it appears that this tragic destruction of the city was not necessary for the Russians to stop and ultimately defeat Napoleon.

Despite the fire, the French troops were able to locate food stored in cellar facilities and lived better in Moscow than they had during their long advance toward the city. All Napoleon's proposals, during his stay in Moscow, to Alexander were ignored. Unfortunately for the French, Napoleon still had not understood Alexander. Like his predecessor, Peter the Great, Alexander was a prag-

Field Marshal Mikhail Kutuzov

Mikhail Kutuzov was born 1745. He served as a military commander under three Russian tsars, Catherine II, Paul I, and Alexander I and led Russian troops in three wars with Turkey. He was in command of the Russian troops at Austerlitz in 1805 and was retired after the Austrian-Russian defeat. He was recalled as commander-in-chief of the Russian Army in August 1812. Although considered a narrow victory for Napoleon, the Battle of Borodino may nonetheless be considered a high point in Kutuzov's career because it demonstrated that Napoleon could be stopped. He suddenly got sick and died in Poland in 1813 while leading the pursuit of the defeated French Army.

matist. He understood Napoleon's objectives, and he knew how to deny them. When Napoleon's enormous army crossed the Niemen into Russian territory, Alexander quickly adjusted his plans from an aggressive push toward Warsaw to adopting Barclay de Tolly's approach of retreat and destruction of all supplies. He was pushed by the nobility in St. Petersburg to defend the Russian soil, so he compromised—he encouraged Barclay to stand and fight, but not too hard. He had to install Kutuzov over Barclay, but he tolerated even Kutuzov's continuous retreat and eventual sacrifice of Moscow. He realized that ultimately this approach would allow Russia to win the war. At the time Napoleon entered Moscow, apparently thinking the war won, Alexander had more reason than ever to think the opposite would happen. Napoleon had lost at least 70 percent of his army, so Alexander saw no need to negotiate.

Because of Napoleon's failure to comprehend Alexander's thinking or even the perilous situation of his own army, every day that Napoleon stayed in Moscow brought the destruction of his army closer. Some historians have suggested that when Napoleon eventually left Moscow in October, he had several options: moving to Kiev for improved supply sources or aiming his remaining army toward St. Petersburg. Such proposals appear rather unrealistic. When Napoleon left Moscow, he no longer had the manpower and other resources to implement aggressive action. His only remaining option was to try to bring the rest of his Grand Army of about ninety-five thousand men out of Russia. That task turned out to be one of the hardest he had ever faced.

During the period Napoleon was waiting for a response from Alexander, Kutuzov's forces were being reinforced by sources from many parts of Russia. As a result, when Napoleon finally decided to leave Moscow and start his retreat west, the numerical advantage had switched to the Russians. Napoleon was no longer the hunter looking for a decisive battle. The French were now the ones hunted, trying to escape under increasingly desperate conditions.

The Retreat

Since it is perfectly clear that when Napoleon left Moscow his campaign had ended in dismal failure, it might seem unnecessary to describe the remaining two months of his campaign. However, the many dramatic events during the devastating French retreat could justify a book by themselves. This account will extend to the amazing escape of the French across the Berezina River at the village of Borisov. Berezina runs north-south about fifty kilometers west of the Dnieper, and Borisov is located six hundred kilometers from Moscow. One hundred years earlier, Peter the Great tried, unsuccessfully, to stop Charles XII from crossing the Berezina.

Napoleon left Moscow on October 19. To reach Smolensk, where significant French food supplies were maintained, he chose the route via Kaluga. A part of Kutuzov's pursuing force intercepted the leading French forces, commanded by Eugene, at a small river near Moscow. After a day of fighting, the Russians withdrew. However, Napoleon feared that Kutuzov's main force was approaching and changed the direction of the retreat to use the route via Borodino, the same route the French had taken during the advance to Moscow in September. This switch resulted in about a week's delay and has been considered by some a bad mistake.

On November 13, Napoleon's diminished army of about forty-five thousand was in Smolensk. The Imperial Guard had just sixteen thousand of the forty-eight thousand men it had in June. Davout's corps had ten thousand of the original seventy-two thousand. Ney's force of thirty-two thousand was reduced to three thousand. Napoleon had lost more than half his fighting force since leaving Moscow, and he was hampered by a mass of deserters, who were no longer of any military use but were following the troops, grabbing and frequently destroying whatever supplies they could find.

On November 16, with the Army around Krasnoi, Napoleon decided to finally employ the Guard in a counterattack. His purpose was to ensure that the main route of retreat for the Grand Army remained open. Kutuzov's forces, which had experienced no aggressive action from the French for several weeks, were caught by surprise. After significant losses, the Russian commander ordered his troops to retreat south. Despite this success, Napoleon began to realize that time was running short to get his dwindling force out of Russia. He needed to find a place of supply to replace Smolensk, and crossing the river Berezina might become a major challenge.

At the start of the campaign in June, Oudinot's Second Corps had been assigned to protect Napoleon's northern flank and prevent Wittgenstein's forces from joining the main Russian Army. While the main French Army completed its advance to Moscow and subsequently commenced its retreat, the Second Corps had been involved in many inconclusive confrontations with Wittgenstein's troops. Oudinot's corps had been reinforced by Marshal Victor's Ninth Corps, but due to more rapid attrition among the French forces and reinforcements to Wittgenstein, in early November, the Russian Northern Army was superior to the two French corps. Oudinot and Victor were supposed to secure the Dvina River line, making Vitebsk, instead of Smolensk, available for Napoleon to provide supply and rest for his half-starving Grand Army. However, Wittgenstein's energetic moves pushed the French forces south after a number of smaller but critical encounters. As a result, Napoleon lost the chance to benefit from the supply in Vitebsk. Wittgenstein's Northern Army had seized the town. Some of his reinforcements had been Russian troops from Finland, made available as a result of Alexander's arrangement with Bernadotte. Minsk had been another possibility, but even that was gone. It had been captured by Admiral Chichagov's Southern Russian Army.

Now Napoleon had to aim for Vilna, and to get his troops there, he had to cross the Berezina River. To move his troops faster, Napoleon ordered all wagons carrying relatively unessential items, including a lot of loot from Moscow, to be destroyed. Unfortunately, he included even wagons carrying equipment for building bridges, assuming that his troops would be able to use the bridge across the Berezina at Borisov or even cross the river on the ice. Napoleon moved quickly to secure the Borisov bridge and left Marshal Ney with six thousand men to hold off Kutuzov. But on November 21, Chichagov got to Borisov first and overwhelmed a small French force guarding the bridge. In addition, the ice on the river turned out to be too weak to allow a crossing. Napoleon was now blocked east of the Berezina.

It very much looked as if a Russian pincer plan, put together in St. Petersburg, would succeed in catching the French Army between Chichagov's force advancing from the southwest, Wittgenstein's troops advancing from the north, and Kutuzov's main Russian Army pursuing Napoleon from the east—a total of about 110,000 against Napoleon's remaining force of about sixty thousand. If the Russian plan had succeeded, what of Waterloo?

With the bridge at Borisov lost, Napoleon originally planned to try crossing the Berezina south of Borisov. A detachment of troops started cutting trees in that area. On November 23, troops from Oudinot's corps discovered a ford at Studienka, about ten kilometers north of Borisov, a far better place than anything located south of Borisov. However, Chichagov, with his forces stationed along the west side of the Berezina as far north as Studienka, prevented any bridge work. With Wittgenstein pushing from the north and Kutuzov approaching from the east, time was running out for the French, but Napoleon rose to the challenge. He dispatched more troops, and even masses of stragglers, to the area where work had been started on the river south of Borisov. Chichagov fell for the ruse. Convinced that the French were going to cross south of Borisov, he removed his troops from Studienka. Napoleon promptly ordered Oudinot to get his troops across the river, using the ford, and to secure a bridgehead west of the river. Oudinot carried out the order so efficiently that he even recaptured Borisov, but the bridge there had been destroyed.

As soon as Oudinot had secured the bridgehead, Napoleon ordered General Eble, head of the engineering group, to start building new bridges. Fortunately, Eble had violated Napoleon's order and kept seven wagons with bridge-building equipment. Without this equipment, the French would have been in an almost hopeless situation. Using their tools, the French engineers worked for twenty-four hours through the night and by midday of November 26 had completed two new bridges. Napoleon himself stayed at the river, encouraging the engineers, many of whom died in the icy water. Before the bridges were completed, the pursuing Russian forces came within artillery range. One bridge was badly damaged and had to be rebuilt. The next day, Napoleon and most of his army crossed the river.

During the critical period of November 23 to 29, Victor was able to keep Wittgenstein's superior forces from advancing to the river. At one dangerous point, Napoleon was able to unleash an artillery barrage, which slowed the advancing Russian forces. Once Victor's rearguard had crossed the river on November 29, General Eble ordered the bridges destroyed. Without access to the bridges, thousands of injured soldiers, stragglers, deserters, and civilians drowned in trying to cross the river or were left on the east side waiting for the Russians and the Cossacks. Some historians have felt that Napoleon's leadership during these critical days was the best of his entire Russian campaign. One wrote, "Buenaparte had here entirely saved his old honour and acquire new, but the result was still a stride towards the utter destruction of the army."[15] Nonetheless, the real heroes on this occasion were General Eble and his engineers. More than half of them died in the river, and Eble himself died within three weeks; but they saved Napoleon, his marshals, and the tiny remnants of the Grand Army.

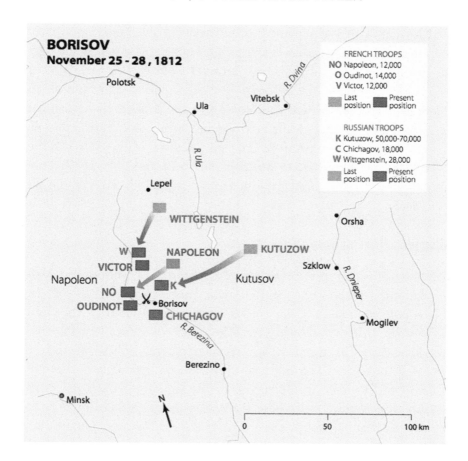

There were some recriminations among the Russians concerning Napoleon's escape. The official position was that Chichagov was the principal culprit, having been misled by French activities to move his troops too far south on the western side of the Berezina. However, it seems fairly clear that both Wittgenstein and Kutuzov failed to advance as fast as they might have. A big share of the blame should be allocated to them.[16]

Napoleon's Campaign Failed. Why?

The outcome of Napoleon's 1812 war against Tsar Alexander must be considered one of the most unlikely and peculiar results of any recorded military campaign. When launching his attack in June

1812, Napoleon was regarded as an exceptionally talented military commander, and his French troops were rated by many as the best in Europe. He started his advance into Russia with a force almost three times as big as the defending Russian armies. However, when Napoleon reached Moscow, following two and one-half months of marching and smaller confrontations and skirmishes, with only one major battle, 70 percent of his fighting force was lost. And when the French troops left Russian territory on December 11, 1812, only ten thousand reasonably healthy troops remained. How was that possible?

Unrealistic Expectations

Before beginning his campaign, Napoleon had announced that he intended to win the conflict with Russia within three weeks. Napoleon wanted to make Russia return to his team in the fight against the British and to impress Alexander enough so that the relationship from the time of the Tilsit agreement in 1807 would be restored. Alexander and other European rulers, particularly those in Austria and Prussia, would recognize the superior French power in Europe. To achieve these objectives, Napoleon needed not only to defeat the Russian troops decisively, he also had to preserve his own forces. At the end of the campaign, France's military power had to be such that its position would be respected.

Napoleon ruined his chances of success right from the start by bringing in an enormous army. Alexander and Barclay de Tolly realized immediately that Russia did not have the troops to stop such an army close to the border. As a result, Napoleon's armies were dragged by the retreating Russian troops first to Drissa, on the Dvina River, then to Vitebsk and finally to Smolensk, and still without a major battle. At Smolensk, only two months into the war in early August 1812, Napoleon's campaign had, in reality, failed. His armies had already suffered such heavy losses that even a decisive victory against Barclay de Tolly followed by cooperative assurances from Alexander would not be enough. It was too late. Napoleon could not return from his Russian campaign with a French force sufficient to convince the major European powers that France was still dominant.

Had Napoleon crossed the Niemen River with a force of about two hundred thousand of his best French troops, the Tsar might well have quickly engaged his army in a major battle. This might have resulted in a decisive victory for Napoleon and persuaded Alexander to sue for peace.

Strategic and Tactical Errors

Napoleon was frustrated by the immediate Russian retreat. As he told the Russian ambassador: "I do not know Barclay de Tolly, but, judging from his first moves in this campaign, he is rather lacking in military talent…"[17] That was a peculiar observation since Barclay's decision would appear to have been the only one he could make to save his army under the circumstances. With his expectations of a quick victory and end of the war dashed within a week or two of its start, what was Napoleon to do? Unlike Charles XII, Napoleon had no established target for his campaign, neither Moscow nor St. Petersburg. He had not planned for an invasion that far into Russia. He hesitated and stayed in Vilna for nearly two weeks. Since it now appeared likely that Barclay would try to avoid a decisive battle, Napoleon might have decided to advance toward St. Petersburg, a target the Russians would have had to defend.

St. Petersburg was at that time the capital of Russia, and it was there you could find the Tsar and all the influential nobility and other elite. It was also the principal trading port. Had he selected this option early in his campaign, he might have accomplished one major objective. Alexander would probably have been forced to make a new commitment to cooperate. However, the costs to the Grand Army would have been such that France's military position in Europe would not have been improved. Nonetheless, Napoleon's decision to continue the pursuit of Barclay's army east was far worse because it offered almost no potential for success.

The pressure on Barclay from the Tsar and the nobility in St. Petersburg offered Napoleon a chance at Vitebsk, but he missed it as a result of his indecision. Following this new disappointment, Napoleon stayed for a couple of weeks in Vitebsk, trying to decide what to do next. Although the campaign had lasted only five weeks, the Grand Army had already suffered greatly by the time it reached Vitebsk. Since conditions were not likely to improve, Napoleon's best option would have been to terminate the campaign, as suggested by Caulaincourt and most of Napoleon's other senior commanders.

A move toward St. Petersburg was still an option that probably would have offered Napoleon a major battle with Barclay. While Napoleon was in Vitebsk, Barclay's First Western Army had joined forces with Bagration's Second Western Army. They were now in the Smolensk area, 130 kilometers east of Vitebsk. If Napoleon had started to move northwest toward St. Petersburg, Alexander would certainly have ordered Barclay to try to stop Napoleon's advance. That could hardly have been done without a major battle, which was what Napoleon was seeking. Nonetheless, the result would have been about the same as if he had gone toward St. Petersburg from Vilna. He might have received cooperation from Alexander, but his already weakened Grand Army would have suffered greater losses than Napoleon could afford. Napoleon hesitated, but in the end, he decided to continue the pursuit of Barclay and Bagration. As at Vilna, he chose the option with the least chance of success.

Nevertheless, the next stage of Napoleon's campaign, Smolensk, provided a new opportunity for him to force a major battle. As at Vitebsk, this opportunity was not created by Napoleon, but by Alexander. Responding to demands by influential groups in St. Petersburg, Alexander told Barclay to become more aggressive. So Barclay started a hesitant move northwest of Smolensk, which created an opportunity for Napoleon to cut off the Russian Army's retreat. Napoleon's plan was fine, but his execution was poor. In addition to taking a day off to celebrate his birthday, he wasted time by an unnecessary and costly attack against the old fortress. As a result, the Russian Army reached the road to Moscow first and escaped. Had Napoleon succeeded in cutting off Barclay's retreat east, Barclay would have had to fight.

Napoleon was now in Smolensk, and his campaign had gone on for two months. It was still summer in Russia, but time was getting short. Napoleon had already lost 40 to 45 percent of his army, and he was still a long way from either Moscow or St. Petersburg. Napoleon again hesitated. After the fact, it seems clear that in Smolensk in August 1812, Napoleon faced a red line that he should not have crossed. This line related to the possible destruction of the Grand Army. It would result from an advance by Napoleon against either Moscow or St. Petersburg. Napoleon's only chance of survival was now to terminate the campaign. He made the wrong choice. He continued to advance in pursuit of Barclay. Every step east toward Moscow did not bring him closer to victory against Alexander, but closer to the total destruction of his own army and ultimately to his position as emperor.

Allied Parties

As a result of Napoleon's victories in 1806–09, he had succeeded in getting both Austrian and Prussian support for his battle with Britain and in his campaign against Russia.[18] They were countries he needed to impress by a quick decisive victory in Russia. There were strong objections in both countries to the alliance with Napoleon. Prussia was in the process of reforming its military, the effectiveness of which had declined substantially since the days of Frederick the Great. When the alliance with France was announced, Generals Scharnhorst and Gneisenau, who held key positions as leaders of the reform effort, both resigned.[19] Either country was likely to desert Napoleon if his Russian campaign went badly, especially if his huge invasion army was lost.[20] Nonetheless, Napoleon seems to have ignored these considerations when he made the decision in Smolensk to continue east.

Napoleon at Borodino and Moscow

Borodino was not one of Napoleon's more brilliant victories. He stationed himself almost three kilometers away from the action and was barely able to follow developments in the battle. Observers felt that he seemed listless and tired. According to some, he fell asleep halfway through the battle. He rejected Davout's possibly effective plan for an encircling move and failed to employ the Imperial Guard at a crucial point late in the battle. If Napoleon had displayed his old mastery at Borodino, the event might have resulted in a far worse defeat for the Russians. Still, it seems unlikely that such a result would have made a significant difference to the outcome of Napoleon's campaign or the eventual fate of France and himself.

A fundamental problem for Napoleon was that he had failed to understand Alexander's attitude. Napoleon apparently assumed that his victory at Borodino, combined with the conquest of Moscow, would make Alexander come to terms. Napoleon should have realized much sooner that he was wrong. He had tried to get Alexander to negotiate during his advance to Moscow. Once in Moscow, Napoleon tried again. Still no negotiation; that is when he should have left Moscow, cutting his stay to maybe a week instead of a month. That would probably not have changed the final outcome of the coming battle between France and its enemies. The decline of the Grand Army had already proceeded too far for that. However, starting the retreat from Moscow three weeks or so, earlier, might have enabled Napoleon to finish his Russian campaign with a remnant of the Grand Army of fifty thousand to seventy-five thousand instead of ten thousand men.

Why So Many Errors?

Napoleon was a highly intelligent, pragmatic individual and an excellent military commander. Why did things in Russia work out so badly? Some historians have suggested that by 1812, Napoleon was burned out. Napoleon had ruled France for thirteen years. Even though he was only forty-three in 1812, it is reasonable to assume that his extreme work schedule and the pressure of almost continuous warfare might have taken a significant toll even on a man with as great energy as Napoleon.[21]

The Russian campaign also forced Napoleon to face conditions very different from those he had dealt with during his successful campaigns in Western Europe. There, his opponents—whether

Austrians, Italians, Prussians, or even Russians—had invariably acted to face his army, often resulting in decisive battles. He also had been able to find sufficient supplies for his army. In Russia, conditions turned out to be quite different. His opponent did not seem ready to defend any part of his huge country, electing to continue a seemingly endless retreat. As a result, Napoleon had been forced to waste his army's strength in a pursuit he had not planned, and for which he did not have adequate resources. The interruptions of his campaign in Vilna, Vitebsk, and Smolensk indicate that he realized that his campaign was not only frustrating but conceivably leading him toward failure. However, each time he stopped to reevaluate matters, even the advice from his most respected commanders was not enough to make him accept the fact that the campaign was failing and that a painful decision was necessary to save his empire.

Napoleon's occasional failure in execution, as at Vitebsk, Smolensk, and, to some extent, at Borodino, might have been caused by his health problems and fatigue along with difficult conditions in Russia. However, his ego was probably the main reason why he failed to make the critical decision to terminate the campaign at Vitebsk or Smolensk. Napoleon was used to almost continuous success and victory. Just as for Charles XII at certain critical points in his Russian campaign, his ego might have prevented the right decision. At Vitebsk and Smolensk, Napoleon apparently considered admitting that his Russian venture had failed. However, his campaign against Alexander had received great publicity. In the end, Napoleon was unable to face the reality of failure and take steps to save his army and his empire. Such a conclusion is supported by General Caulaincourt's account of how he, Marshal Berthier, and several other commanders tried unsuccessfully at Vitebsk to convince Napoleon to terminate the campaign. Instead of listening to their advice, Napoleon indulged in "illusions and wishful thinking."[22]

There remains the question of why Napoleon failed to recognize that St. Petersburg, rather than Moscow, should have been the campaign's target once it was clear that Barclay would not do battle near the border. Transportation and supply aspects would have made St. Petersburg easier to reach. Most importantly, it was a location that Alexander could not afford to lose. Napoleon's failure to target St. Petersburg was a fundamental error. When he was staying in Smolensk to await Alexander's response to proposals for negotiations, Napoleon's situation had already deteriorated drastically. He had already lost half his army. The Russian Army remained a viable force, having incurred far smaller losses than the French. In reality, Napoleon had accomplished next to nothing and had performed almost exactly as Alexander might have wished.

If Napoleon instead had gone from Vilna toward St. Petersburg two months into the campaign, St. Petersburg, if not already conquered, would have been under such threat that the Tsar would have had to negotiate. So why did Napoleon persist in going in the wrong direction? This issue did not require an admission of failure, so ego would not have prevented Napoleon from the right choice. Rather it seems he acted like a gambler.[23] He started out determined to defeat the Russian Army. Barclay refused to fight near the border, so Napoleon hoped he would fight at the fortress at Drissa on the Dvina River. Barclay would not fight there either, but retreats to Vitebsk. So Napoleon goes on to Vitebsk. Barclay escapes to Smolensk without almost any fight. Napoleon goes to Smolensk. Barclay again escapes. Napoleon is caught like a gambler in wishful thinking: if he only hangs on a little longer, he will win. This approach eventually caused the destruction of the French Army.[24]

The harsh Russian winter played a big role in the hardships and the losses the French and Russian armies suffered during Napoleon's retreat. However, the outcome of Napoleon's 1812 campaign had been decided long before the retreat began.

CHARLES XII AND
THE GREAT NORTHERN WAR

Turning from Napoleon in 1812 to Charles XII about one hundred years earlier, there are both similarities and distinct differences between their two campaigns.

Military Action

The Attack on Sweden

The Great Northern War started when an allied group—Denmark, Saxony, and Russia—attacked Sweden in 1700. They wanted to recover land lost to Sweden in previous wars. They felt the premature death of Charles XI, a strong ruler, created an opportunity. His son, Charles XII, had been sworn in as king at the age of fifteen, two years before the three allies attacked. It seemed logical to assume that he would have little capacity to govern the country, let alone deal with an attack by three powerful neighbors.

Sweden was considered the most powerful nation in Northern Europe at the time. Besides Sweden proper, Finland, what is now St. Petersburg, the Baltic countries and a number of port cities in Northern Germany were Swedish territory. Some of these areas became part of Sweden following the 1648 Westphalian peace treaty that ended the thirty-year war. Other parts were conquered by Charles X Gustav and Charles XI, Charles XII's grandfather and father. Sweden had a well-trained army based on an unusual system, under which big landowners had to supply and support a certain number of soldiers for the king. The Swedish Navy controlled the northern part of the Baltic Sea, from the southern tip of Gotland all the way north to the end of the sea.

However, Sweden was a poor country with meager agricultural conditions, so severe that occasionally peasants were forced to mix bark in the bread to feed themselves. In many of the wars involving Sweden from approximately 1630 to 1710, the Swedish forces were subsidized by the French, who every now and then found the Swedish Army a useful tool to support various French ambitions. For a big power, Sweden had a small population—only around two million inhabitants. In comparison, both France and Russia had populations of fifteen to twenty million. Despite its strong army, Sweden's position as a big power in Europe was precarious.

King Charles XII

Charles XII was crowned king of Sweden at age fifteen in 1697 and ruled until his death in 1718. Because of his early and continuous engagements in military activities, his capability as a civilian adminis-trator was hardly tested, but he showed himself an excellent leader of troops in battle. He even had a good understanding of strategy and logistical planning. However, he frequently acted in a reckless and immature fashion in respect to the interests of Sweden and the safety of his soldiers and himself. To a large extent, this was probably the result of Charles getting absolute powers over Sweden's people and assets at such an exceptionally early age. Charles listened patiently to suggestions by his commanders, but he hardly ever adopted any of their advice. His disdain for his opponents, particularly the Russians, was a major cause of Sweden's eventual misfortunes.

In responding to the three allies' attacks in 1700, Charles quickly proved their expectations wrong. Within months of the attacks, he invaded the Danish Islands, aided by British and Dutch fleets, and forced Denmark to sign a peace treaty. Charles then turned on Russia. Peter the Great had begun a siege of Narva, a key Swedish fortress on the eastern side of the Baltic. In the fall of 1700 following his Danish victory, Charles brought a Swedish Army across the Baltic and completed a strenuous march to Narva. The Swedish troops, outnumbered four or five to one, immediately attacked and inflicted a devastating defeat on Peter's forces.

Charles then took on his third enemy, his first cousin, August, the regent of Saxony and elected king of Poland. This project required a lot more time, and it was not until the fall of 1706 that Charles had succeeded in getting August to sign a peace treaty. In the meantime, Charles's selected candidate had been elected king of Poland.

During these years, Peter had implemented crucial changes in the Russian military: better training of officers and troops and great improvements in military equipment, especially artillery, which was now manufactured for the first time in Russia. Peter had brought in numerous foreign experts to serve in both the military and civilian administrations.

Peter had also scored significant victories against Swedish troops in the Baltic. He had conquered the Swedish fortresses on Lake Ladoga and reached the Baltic. He had also begun constructing a fortress and eventually a city on the Baltic, which he named St. Petersburg. From very early in his reign, Peter had decided that securing a warm-water port or ports for Russia should be a priority. When he became ruler of Russia, the country's only port was Archangels, which for much of the year was frozen and of no use for naval traffic.

The Start of Charles's Campaign

When it became clear that Charles was about to turn his armies against Russia, Peter tried to reach a peace agreement with Sweden. He enlisted a number of major European countries to help in this effort and was prepared to make substantial concessions. The only thing he would not give up was St. Petersburg. While only a primitive fortress in 1707, Peter saw it being developed into a major trading port. Charles, however, would not consider peace without the return of the land now occupied by St. Petersburg. In addition, Charles felt Peter could not be trusted and should be punished for having attacked Sweden in 1700. So in August 1707, with a Swedish Army of about thirty-five thousand stationed in Altranstad, Saxony, Charles began his campaign.

Charles had a choice between Moscow and St. Petersburg as the target of his campaign. Most of his commanders assumed he would select St. Petersburg. Eventually, it became clear that Moscow was his objective. As in the case of Napoleon, Charles made the wrong choice. St. Petersburg would have been a far more suitable target. Riga, located on the Baltic 480 kilometers from St. Petersburg, was still Swedish, and Sweden controlled this part of the Baltic. So if Charles had moved his army to Riga, it could have been well supplied and reinforced. Peter, on the other hand, faced substantial logistical problems in maintaining troops in the St. Petersburg area.

Tsar, Peter the Great

Peter was born in 1672 and became sole ruler of Russia in 1696. Unlike previous Russian rulers, he had an intense interest in foreign countries, and spent two years in the early part of his reign in Holland and England to learn shipbuilding and other technologies that might be of use in Russia. He brought a large number of foreign experts back to Russia to help him implement his ideas for improving Russia's civilian administration as well as many aspects of its military, including creating Russia's first navy. Peter was pragmatic and a rather cautious commander, although quite willing to expose himself to danger. Unlike Charles, he sought advice from his commanders and frequently followed their suggestions.

That area was located far from other Russian population centers and the road system to the rest of Russia was poorly developed.

Nonetheless, since St. Petersburg and access to the Baltic were Peter's top priorities, it is reasonable to assume that he would have applied all forces at his disposal to avoid losing this area. Charles likely would have gained the opportunity of a decisive battle on favorable terms.

Charles did not announce his destination, and it was not clear at first whether he was aiming for St. Petersburg or Moscow. Both meant a long march, first through Poland where the Swedes were opposed at every significant river crossing by Russian troops. From the start, Peter adopted a strategy of avoiding any major battle, while delaying the enemy as much as possible. This strategy included a ruthless scorched-earth policy. The poor Polish farmers were forced to leave their farms and hide in the woods. Nonetheless, Charles was able to cross all the obstacles without major losses. In January 1708 a troop of Swedish cavalry, led by Charles himself, reached Grodno on the Niemen River, just east of the Polish border. About two thousand Russian cavalry, more than twice the number of Charles's force, were stationed east of the river, but the bridge was not destroyed.

Charles immediately attacked, and after an intense battle, the Russians retreated into the city. This type of quick action, when an opportunity occurred, was something Charles had done successfully in the past. It stands in contrast to Napoleon's hesitation at Vitebsk, which cost him the chance for a possibly decisive battle. Had Charles hesitated at Grodno, the German general commanding the Russian cavalry would probably have destroyed the bridge. Unbeknownst to Charles, Peter was in Grodno at the time. Peter assumed that the aggressive attack indicated that the main Swedish Army was near, so he ordered all Russian troops out of Grodno and began retreating to Vilna.

When the Swedish Army proceeded east rather than north out of Grodno, everyone concerned realized that Charles was aiming for Moscow. Charles established winter quarters for his army near Minsk. While there, he was visited by General Adam Ludwig Lewenhaupt, the commander of Riga, the last major Swedish outpost in the Baltic.

Charles's Plans for Supplies

Having experienced the effects of Peter's scorched-earth policy, Charles realized that he was not going to reach Moscow without supplies from Swedish sources. Riga was the logical choice, so Lewenhaupt received instructions to put together and deliver to a point on the Dnieper River a supply convoy sufficient to provide for the needs of an army of forty thousand for six weeks. The big task of organizing such a convoy and having it start to move east had to be done as quickly as possible. Charles provided Lewenhaupt few details or indications of the ultimate goal of the Russian campaign.

Some of Charles's generals and Carl Piper, the acting Swedish prime minister who accompanied the campaign, were unhappy with Moscow as the campaign's target.

They felt St. Petersburg would be a better choice. Lewenhaupt was persuaded to make a presentation to Charles arguing for a change in plans. Charles listened politely but, as was his habit, refrained from expressing his reaction. Lewenhaupt managed to convince himself that Charles had been persuaded by his suggestions. As a result, he did not expedite the supply convoy's departure as Charles had directed. Instead, he delayed, hoping for new orders that never came. Charles had no intention of departing from his plan to aim for Moscow. Lewenhaupt's delay turned out to be most unfortunate due to circumstances that Lewenhaupt could hardly have predicted.

The Battle of Holowczyn

In late spring of 1708, Charles resumed the march east. Assuming that Charles would try to cross the Berezina River by the bridge at Borisov, Peter had stationed some six thousand troops to defend the bridge. As he had done in Poland, Charles found a different route and crossed the river at the little town of Berezina, some forty kilometers south of Borisov. Peter's two senior commanders, Marshal Boris Sheremetev and General Alexander Menshikov, then decided, with Peter's consent, to risk a major battle to stop Charles's advance. They concentrated forty thousand Russian troops, supported by Cossack forces, along a couple of minor rivers, Drut and Babich, near the town of Holowczyn. Menshikov with ten thousand cavalry was placed farthest north, along the Babich, then Sheremetev with ten thousand infantry. South of Sheremetev's forces, separated by a narrow marsh, were another ten thousand Russian infantry under the command of General Repnin, and south of him a substantial cavalry force commanded by General von der Goltz. This time, Charles decided to accept the challenge and moved up a force of twenty thousand. He concluded that Repnin's section, although protected by the shallow Babich and the marsh, was the best point to attack.

At 6:00 a.m. on July 4, Charles, at the head of eight thousand infantry soldiers, waded across the Babich and through the marshland and attacked Repnin's force. The Russians fought harder than Charles had expected, but finally had to retreat. Von der Goltz's cavalry squadrons tried to support Repnin by attacking the Swedish right flank. However, Field Marshal Carl Gustav Rehnskjöld led the Swedish cavalry across the Babich in a vigorous attack against the Russian cavalry. Although far superior in numbers, the Russian cavalry was eventually chased off the field. The Swedes' victory was impressive but not decisive. The Russian Army was not destroyed and retreated in good order.

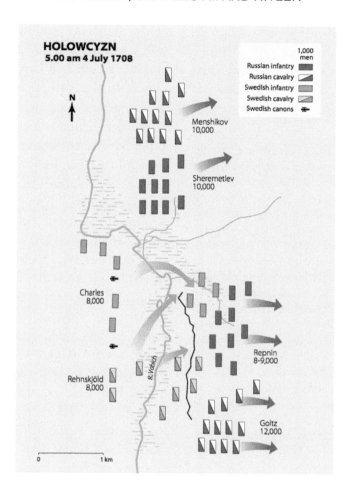

Awaiting Lewenhaupt

Charles's army continued its march east and crossed the Dnieper in early July. The army then made small moves up and down the east side of the river, awaiting Lewenhaupt's arrival. They were engaged in skirmishes with Peter's forces, who tried to make things uncomfortable for the Swedes while still avoiding any major confrontations. In early September, Charles's army was stationed in a little Russian town, Tatarsk, about forty kilometers east of the Dnieper.

Lewenhaupt's supply train consisted of four thousand wagons, each weighing four tons. Lewenhaupt needed nearly three months to move 650 kilometers from Riga on the Baltic to Szklow on the Dnieper. The convoy at times had been stretched over one hundred kilometers. The Swedish victory at Holowczyn allowed Lewenhaupt to advance without any interference from Russian troops. However, due to poor roads, bad weather, equipment breakdowns, and other adverse circumstances, the march had taken far longer than either Lewenhaupt or Charles had expected. Lewenhaupt's groups did not cross the Dnieper until September 23.

> **General Lewenhaupt**
>
> Adam Ludwig Lewenhaupt was born in 1659. At that time, service in foreign armies was the best option for young officers in Sweden. Lewenhaupt served first with the Austrians and then with the Dutch. When he returned to Sweden in 1697, he was commissioned a colonel. Lewenhaupt had great skills in leading troops in battle, and in 1705, as commander of forces in Riga, defeated a far superior Russian army. Following the Battle of Poltava and Charles's flight to the Ottoman Empire, Lewenhaupt was left in charge of the remnant of the Swedish army. He accepted Menshikov's terms of surrender at Perevolochna in July 1709, an act that Charles would never forgive. Lewenhaupt died a prisoner in Moscow in 1719.

Charles, who had expected Lewenhaupt to arrive in early August, had become increasingly impatient. Russia's scorched-earth policy made any farther move toward Moscow impossible without Lewenhaupt's supplies. Just keeping troops and animals fed, where they were, was getting more difficult. In addition, Charles had received a proposal from Ivan Mazepa, hetman (head) of the principal Cossack nation east of the Dnieper, to join the Swedish campaign. The Cossacks were under ultimate Russian rule, but enjoyed substantial autonomy. Mazepa and some other Cossack leaders had become increasingly unhappy over what they considered Peter's high-handed infringements of their rights. Mazepa now was prepared to switch sides and offered Charles substantial support in manpower as well as supplies. However, he wanted Charles to come as quickly as possible to Baturin, his capital in northern Ukraine, approximately 350 kilometers southeast of Tatarsk.

After some discussions with Piper and Rehnskjöld, who felt the army should move toward the Dnieper to meet Lewenhaupt, Charles decided to go south into the Ukraine and eventually toward Baturin.

He knew that Peter had significant forces in the general area of Szklow, the little town where Lewenhaupt was expected to cross the Dnieper. There was a clear danger that Peter, who commanded some of the Russian troops himself, might try to intersect Lewenhaupt's crucial convoy. But Charles believed Lewenhaupt had enough troops (twelve thousand to twenty thousand, according to Charles's estimates) to defeat any Russian attack. He sent messengers to Lewenhaupt, advising him to unite with the main army at the town of Starodub, about two hundred kilometers southeast of Szklow.

Charles left Tatarsk on his move south on September 15, eight days before Lewenhaupt reached Szklow. On September 20, Peter and his senior commanders decided to intercept Lewenhaupt's supply train. Peter instructed Marshal Sheremetev, who was in charge of the biggest part of the army (about forty-five thousand), to monitor Charles's army on its way south into the Ukraine, but to avoid any major confrontations. Peter and Menshikov commanded a force of about fifteen thousand, a combination of cavalry, infantry, and some artillery. They would immediately move toward the point where Lewenhaupt was assumed to have crossed the Dnieper.

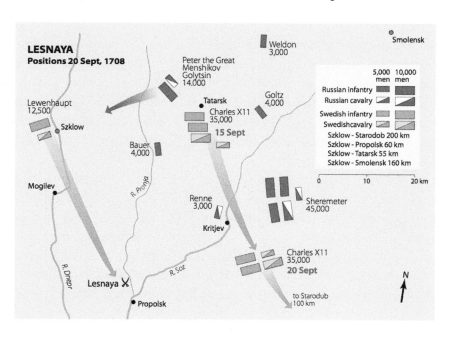

Smaller Russian forces—one of about four thousand under General Frederick Bauer (a former officer in the Swedish Army) stationed only about fifty kilometers east of Szklow and another commanded by General Weldon stationed farther north near Smolensk—were to join Peter's force.

The Battle of Lesnaya

On September 23, Peter's troops made contact with Lewenhaupt's rearguard in the little village of Belitza. Lewenhaupt had realized, the moment he received Charles's new orders, that he would be vulnerable to Russian attack. In addition to the four thousand wagons and personnel to operate, maintain, and repair them, he possessed twelve thousand soldiers, about half of them cavalry and some artillery. He did not know how big an army might try to intercept him, but expected it to be substantially bigger than his force. He had to cross the Soz River, a major tributary to the Dnieper, to reach Starodub. If he could cross the Soz before getting into a major fight with the Russians, he assumed that his supply convoy would be reasonably safe. So following his first contact with Peter's troops, Lewenhaupt pushed his clumsy mass of people, animals, and wagons to move as fast as possible toward the town of Propolsk on the Soz. On September 28, the convoy halted at the little town of Lesnaya on the Lesnjanka River, about ten kilometers west of Propolsk. In the early morning of September 29, Peter and Menshikov began the advance from the west, Peter leading eight thousand infantry on trails through the woods and Menshikov with seven thousand cavalry on the road toward Lesnaya.

At the initial contact between the two armies, most of Lewenhaupt's convoy was still stationed on a big field in Lesnaya, immediately west of the Lesnjanka River. Some advance forces were in Propolsk and some of the wagons, accompanied by some of the troops, were on the road toward Propolsk. Initially, only a small infantry force of about three thousand was facing the advancing Russian Army. The Swedes immediately attacked Peter's troops emerging on the forest trails and almost forced them into a panicky retreat. However, as more of Peter's infantry and Menshikov's cavalry arrived, the Swedish troops were forced to retreat.

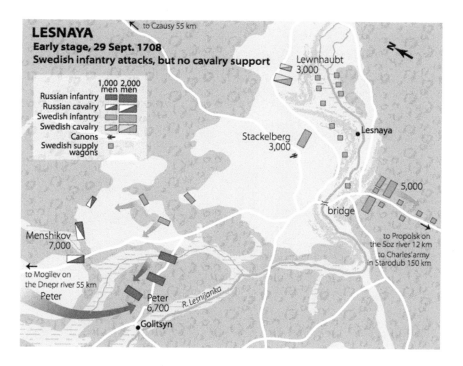

With reinforcements arriving gradually on both sides, the battle went on until the middle of the afternoon. Neither side was able to gain the upper hand. By four o'clock, General Bauer's force of four thousand joined the battle, and Peter's reinforced troops came close to victory. However, a small Swedish cavalry troop, returning from Propolsk, again turned the battle into a stalemate before darkness caused fighting to end.

Although the Swedish troops held their positions on the field, Lesnaya would prove a disaster for the Swedes. Lewenhaupt assumed that the superior Russian troops would resume their attacks the next morning, so to save his force, he started evacuating his positions in the dark of night and moved east toward Propolsk. However, he could not possibly bring along the wagons with the indispensable supplies for Charles's army. Lewenhaupt succeeded in saving a portion of his troops, but when he reached the main Swedish Army ten days later, he only had a force of six thousand exhausted soldiers and no provisions.

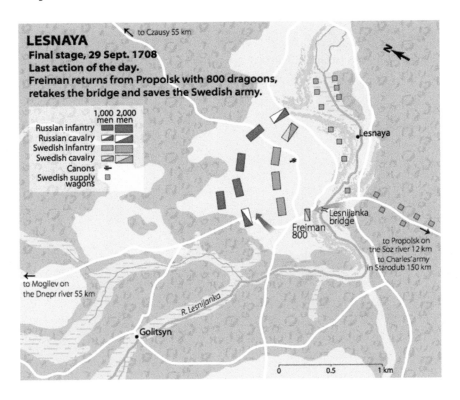

Causes and Consequences of Lesnaya

The principal cause of the Lesnaya disaster was unquestionably Charles' decision to move south toward the Ukraine on September 15. Had he stayed in Tatarsk another week or ten days or moved his army west toward the Dnieper, Peter would not have been able to intersect Lewenhaupt. Charles felt Lewenhaupt had enough troops to defend his convoy, but he did not know the exact troop strength on either side. He did know that Lewenhaupt's supplies were indispensible if he was to continue his campaign. Thus his decision was a disastrous error and one that could not be corrected. It was, as the British military historian J.F.C. Fuller noted, "strategic insanity"[25].

Some observers have felt that Lewenhaupt should have been better prepared for the Russian advance on September 29 since contact had been made already on the twenty-seventh. With a stronger Swedish defensive force on the fields west of Lesnaya, Peter might have been defeated before his troops were even fully lined up for attack. Nonetheless, the principal responsibility rests with Charles.

Since he began his campaign in Altranstädt in October 1707 until he left Tatarsk on September 15, 1708, Charles had moved his army with great skill, avoided the obstacles Peter and nature had presented, and advanced 1,400 kilometers with modest losses. If Lewenhaupt had met up with Charles with his supply convoy intact, the march toward Moscow might well have succeeded. However, Lesnaya changed the situation completely.

While Mazepa's Cossacks might at first have seemed an alternate solution, Peter's fast and decisive moves thwarted that possibility very quickly. Mazepa wanted Charles to come to Baturin to complete the agreement with the Cossack nation and provide protection against Russian forces. However, Mazepa had become nervous that his plan to join the Swedes might have been disclosed to Peter because he had enemies within his own camp. So to protect himself, Mazepa left Baturin with two thousand warriors and went to Charles's camp. Peter had, in fact, become suspicious of Mazepa and had dispatched Menshikov to monitor activities in Baturin. Menshikov discovered that Mazepa had left and reported it to Peter. Peter ordered Menshikov to return to Baturin and ensure that the Cossacks stayed loyal to Russia. Menshikov executed the order with speed, efficiency, and ruthlessness. An estimated fifteen thousand warriors and civilians were killed. The Cossacks were forced to appoint a new hetman, and Baturin was razed.

Options following Lesnaya

Charles arrived at Baturin in early November, barely a month following Lesnaya and within a week or so of Menshikov's "enforcement" visit. Now there was nothing left for the Swedes—no supplies, no reinforcements of Mazepa's little force, not even a town. So if Charles had not been inclined to reevaluate his plans immediately following Lewenhaupt's news about the Lesnaya disaster, certainly the time to do so had arrived when the Swedish Army entered Baturin.

With both Lewenhaupt's and the Cossacks' supplies lost, there was no longer any realistic possibility for Charles to advance toward Moscow. Peter, who understood the new situation perfectly, had gained control of the conflict. Before Lesnaya, wherever Charles went, Peter had to monitor and slow or block the Swedish advance. Now Charles could no longer force Peter to act.

Charles essentially had two options. One was to move his army back to Riga, give the troops some rest, get supplies and reinforcement from Sweden, and begin an attack against St. Petersburg in the spring of 1709. The return from Baturin would have been arduous. Supplies would have remained a problem, and the Army would have encountered enemy skirmishes and various natural obstacles. However, Charles had demonstrated that he could successfully deal with most of these types of problems, and there likely would have been far less interference by major Russian forces than during the Swedish advance from Altranstädt. Peter would hardly have risked any bigger battle to prevent a Swedish retreat.

His other option was to pursue Peter's forces farther into the Ukraine in the hope that Peter would have to engage in a decisive battle. Charles apparently felt this option was justified by the possibility that the Ottoman Empire might enter the war. According to some historians, Charles saw himself as the commander of a joint Swedish-Turkish Army that would march toward Moscow. The Ottomans had reason to dislike Peter, who had gained access to entry into the Black Sea in a peace treaty with the Ottomans in 1698. Swedes and Russians lobbied hard in Constantinople for the Turks to enter or stay out of the war, respectively. The Russians won the lobbying effort. Charles and his top commanders, Rehnskjöld, Lewenhaupt, and Piper, learned a few days before the Battle of Poltava, on June 24, 1709, that the Ottomans would not enter the war.

However, even if the Turks had joined against Peter, it is questionable how much it would have helped Sweden. The Ottomans would have concentrated on retaking the town of Azov and keeping the Russians out of the Black Sea by blocking their entrance to the Lake of Azov. Such actions might have saved the Swedish Army because Peter would probably have sacrificed Poltava in order to protect the Russian position on the Lake of Azov. However, Turkish entry into the war would not have improved the desperate Swedish supply situation. Without supplies, there was little the Swedish Army could have done to coordinate with an Ottoman attack. Certainly, an advance toward Moscow would not have been remotely possible. Such an effort would have been of little interest to the Ottomans leaders, considering that Moscow is located 950 kilometers north of Azov.

Charles's Decision

Reviewing Charles's alternatives in Baturin in early November 1708, there was really only one choice that might have enabled him to win the war against Russia: move the army to Riga. Unfortunately for Sweden, Charles persisted in his pursuit of Peter. The Swedish campaign in Russia went on for another eight months following Charles's disappointing entry into Baturin. However, once Charles decided to continue his advance in the Ukraine following his visit to Baturin, all major strategic decisions had been made. What followed was almost inevitable. While the campaign would not necessarily have needed to end with the disaster at Poltava the chances of any significant victory were extremely slight following Charles's choice in Baturin.

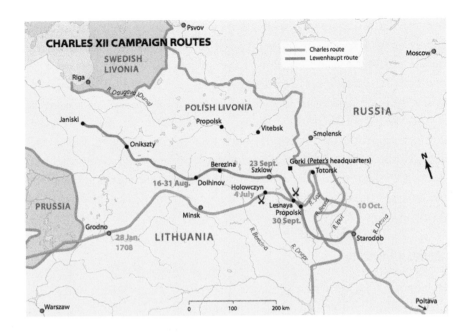

Assessments and Comparisons

Charles's Performance

It is easier to understand Charles's actions and maneuvers than those of Napoleon, because Charles performed about as one might have expected. His ego, immaturity, youth, and failure to properly assess Peter and his troops explain his decisions fairly well. In Altranstädt in the early fall of 1707, Charles undoubtedly realized that St. Petersburg was his best target for a campaign against Peter, but he was confident he could do whatever he pleased. He liked the possibility of humiliating Peter by going all the way to Moscow and either making Peter comply with all his demands or replacing him. So he chose Moscow.

In Tartarsk in September 1708, Charles was impatient and irritated by Lewenhaupt's slow progress. He also hated retreats. He told Rehnskjöld and Piper that a move toward the Dnieper to meet Lewenhaupt would look like a retreat and suggest that he had wasted two months going back and forth east of the Dnieper. Just as

Napoleon's ego kept him from making the right decisions at Vitebsk and Smolensk, Charles's ego caused him to make perhaps the worst decision of his career.

A month later, Charles was in Baturin, and it was obvious that Mazepa could provide next to nothing to help his campaign. One might excuse Charles for wanting to explore the Cossack alternative before making a fundamental evaluation of how to proceed. But following his arrival at Baturin, the time to decide had arrived. He had no supplies, and he was to get none from Mazepa. A restart in Riga was now the only option for success. It was probably Charles's ego that again prevented him from admitting that his campaign to defeat Peter had failed, and that he now had to start over. The possibility that the Ottoman Empire might join the war became his excuse for making the wrong decision and pursuing Peter farther into the Ukraine.

Napoleon was in a similar position in Smolensk in August 1812. He knew then that any farther advance would likely lead to disaster. Nonetheless, after long hesitation and despite strong advice by his commanders to terminate the campaign, Napoleon decided to pursue Barclay.

Charles and Napoleon: Similarities in Strategies

Following Baturin, Charles's approach had significant similarities to Napoleon's continued quest of the Russian Army following Vitebsk and Smolensk. The Swedish and the French leaders were both pursuing an enemy in the belief—just a hope, really—that sooner or later the enemy would have to stop, fight, and be defeated. What they failed to realize was that the enemy did not have to fight unless it considered it advantageous, because neither the Swedish nor the French Army could threaten any target the enemy deemed essential to defend. In the meantime, both attacking armies suffered badly from lack of supplies, causing disease and starvation among soldiers and animals as well as an increase in desertion. To defeat the enemy, whether Napoleon or Charles, all the Russians had to do was to retreat and watch the attackers gradually bleed to death.

Napoleon had established Moscow as the goal a few weeks into his campaign. He believed, inaccurately, that Moscow was crucial to Tsar Alexander. On his entry into Baturin, Charles could only conclude that any prospect of an advance to Moscow was lost. Following that conclusion, Charles appears to have had no clear target or strategy except keeping his army in the Ukraine for possible cooperation with the Ottomans—not a promising strategy. He made matters worse by failing to secure a route for reinforcements or retreat. Since Charles's strategy no longer included any geographic target, he had flexibility in selecting his headquarters. Perevulochna on the Dnieper might have been an option. Since he had chosen to wait for the Ottoman decision, there was time to establish necessary crossing facilities of the Dnieper for reinforcements (expected from Swedish forces in Poland) or for Charles's army if a retreat became desirable.

The Preservation of Forces

Charles succeeded in preserving his army far better than did Napoleon. Charles's fateful decision at Tatarsk took place eleven months following the start of his campaign, after the Army had covered 1,400 kilometers and engaged in one major and numerous smaller battles. Nonetheless, the Army still retained about 80 percent of the soldiers, who had started out in Altranstädt, Saxony. Only a fourth of Napoleon's army remained when he entered Moscow in an operation that had lasted less than three months and included only one major battle.

At Poltava in June 1709, Charles's campaign had gone on for twenty-one months. His army had somehow survived two Russian winters, the second one of exceptional severity. His army had suffered greatly, but 40 to 45 percent of the soldiers were still serving. The Swedish Army remained an effective fighting force. In fact, it appeared so effective that on June 26, 1709, when the Swedish Army lined up on a field in front of the fortified Russian camp two kilometers north of Poltava, Peter chose not to allow his army—more than twice the size of the Swedish one—to leave its fortified camp and meet the Swedes on the open field.

As for the French cavalry, it was for all practical purposes eliminated a few weeks into the retreat from Moscow. At Smolensk in November 1812, only 4,500 horsemen remained out of some 80,000 at the start of the campaign. As Napoleon himself reported, many former horsemen were walking.[26]

In contrast, even at Poltava, the Swedish cavalry was superior to its Russian counterpart, which had to seek protection by the artillery in the Russian camp to avoid being destroyed by the Swedes.

The Command Structures

Napoleon and Charles led their armies in quite different ways. Because of the size of armies at the beginning of the nineteenth century, no single individual could direct or control all actions. Napoleon had established the corps system to deal with this problem. A corps was a unit of around twenty thousand or more infantry, cavalry, and some artillery. If necessary, it could act on its own as a small army. It was commanded by a senior officer, who reported directly to the commander-in-chief. Napoleon's bigger battles usually involved five or six corps, each commanded by one of his marshals. To successfully implement Napoleon's plans of battle, it was essential that the different marshals responded promptly and efficiently to Napoleon's directions, usually conveyed by a courier. With Napoleon at his highly efficient level of command, the system had worked well, but one might wonder what would happen if Napoleon suddenly would not be able to direct his army.

During the first two months of the Russian campaign in 1812, the corps were operating far apart. Who could take over the place of Napoleon? All the marshals were highly competitive and had big egos. There was a good deal of strife and disagreement among them. None was designated as the one to take over and be obeyed. Fortunately for the French, Napoleon stayed in command, although often not at his most efficient level.

Invading Russia in 1708–09, the Swedish Army at peak strength never amounted to more than about forty-five thousand, less than 10 percent of Napoleon's army, when crossing the Niemen River in June

1812. Charles exercised complete, unquestioned authority. Field Marshal Rehnskjöld was second in the military structure and General Lewenhaupt was third. With the Swedish Army of such modest size, this command structure should have functioned well. However, it really did not, primarily because neither Charles nor Rehnskjöld appreciated the need to keep subordinate commanders sufficiently informed of plans, even when a complicated battle was anticipated. In addition, Rehnskjöld and Lewenhaupt had a very poor working relationship.

Charles had acquired so dominant a position that, when he suddenly became incapacitated ten days before Poltava in June 1709, his obvious successor, Rehnskjöld, was unable or unwilling to exercise effective command. As a result, during these critical days before the battle, the Swedish Army failed to take advantage of opportunities that might have prevented Peter's troops from getting an extremely favorable position. In the end, this failure to act made the Swedish command launch an attack despite absurdly unfavorable odds. Because of Peter's careful defensive preparations, the Swedish plan of attack against an enemy drastically superior in manpower and in a fortified camp had to be very complicated. Perfect execution was required for success.

Nonetheless, General Lewenhaupt, second in command in Charles's absence, was not included in planning the attack. This was a serious error because Lewenhaupt had been designated to command the infantry, and the infantry was meant to play a decisive role in the attack. According to one analyst, Rehnskjöld did not fully inform Lewenhaupt because he was afraid of encountering objections.[27] Several major generals, commanding critical parts of the attacking force, were also left in the dark concerning specifics of the plan. The result is illustrated in the two maps of the early stages of the Poltava battle. The first shows the situation after the initial hour or two of advance, as planned by Charles and Rehnskjöld. The second shows the actual situation. At about 6:00 a.m., the main Russian infantry force was still in its camp and had not confronted the Swedes. Nonetheless, there can be little doubt that the Swedes had already lost the battle. It is hard to imagine a better example of how top command may fail in its responsibility to develop and convey a plan of battle.

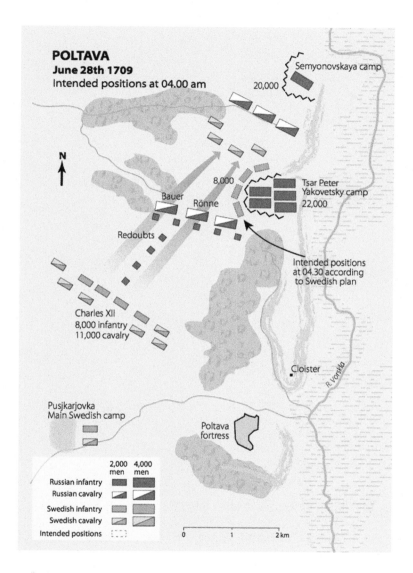

POLTAVA
June 28th 1709
Intended positions at 04.00 am

Semyonovskaya camp
20,000

Bauer
Rönne
8,000
Redoubts

Tsar Peter
Yakovetsky camp
22,000

Intended positions
at 04.30 according
to Swedish plan

Charles XII
8,000 infantry
11,000 cavalry

Cloister
R. Vorskla

Pusjkarjovka
Main Swedish camp

Poltava
fortress

2,000 4,000
men   men
Russian infantry
Russian cavalry
Swedish infantry
Swedish cavalry
Intended positions

0   1   2 km

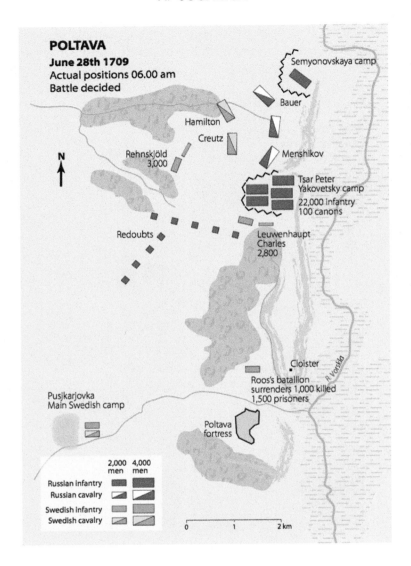

POLTAVA

June 28th 1709
Actual positions 06.00 am
Battle decided

Semyonovskaya camp

Bauer

Hamilton

Creutz

Rehnskjöld
3,000

Menshikov

N

Tsar Peter
Yakovetsky camp

22,000 infantry
100 canons

Redoubts

Leuwenhaupt
Charles
2,800

Cloister

Roos's batallion
surrenders 1,000 killed
1,500 prisoners

R. Vorskla

Pusjkarjovka
Main Swedish camp

Poltava
fortress

	2,000 men	4,000 men
Russian infantry		
Russian cavalry		
Swedish infantry		
Swedish cavalry		

0   1   2 km

Enemy Evaluation of Napoleon and Charles

The top Russian command appears to have looked on Napoleon and Charles quite differently. Even before starting his campaign, Napoleon tried hard to get into negotiations with Tsar Alexander. Napoleon maintained these efforts during his long stay in Moscow. Alexander, however, refused to respond. Some of Napoleon's approaches, while in Moscow, were conveyed through Kutuzov, who received Napoleon's messengers politely. But he advised Alexander in St Petersburg to ignore the French suggestions. Kutuzov had obviously recognized that Napoleon had lost so much strength, that he no longer was in a position to make any demands.

In contrast, from the time Charles was getting ready for his campaign in the fall of 1707, Peter the Great tried continuously to reach a negotiated peace with Sweden. Peter promised to return all territory taken from Sweden in the Baltic provinces after 1700, except St. Petersburg. In compensation for taking the land, on which St. Petersburg was being built, Peter was willing to pay an indemnity. Charles said no.

Even during the Swedish campaign, the Russian peace efforts continued. Menshikov conveyed the latest shortly before the battle of Poltava. It appears that the different attitudes to peace efforts by Peter and Alexander reflected differing assessments of the dangers presented by the French and the Swedish forces. It might at first seem unlikely, but Napoleon's huge force scared Alexander far less than Charles's smaller force did Peter. This was demonstrated in the actions in the field. While Alexander canceled his intended attack on Warsaw, once he realized the size of Napoleon's army, he kept pushing Barclay de Tolly to stop retreating and launch counterattacks at Vitebsk and Smolensk. When Napoleon started his retreat from Moscow, the Russian high command was dedicated to the pursuit and destruction of the French Army. Its respect for Napoleon was by then drastically reduced.

Peter, on the other hand, maintained his strategy of avoiding a major confrontation with the Swedes. He clearly realized that eventually the Swedish Army would be so weakened, by small skirmishes, lack of adequate supplies and the absence of reinforcements, that a forceful Russian stand would succeed. The principal reason for the Russian efforts to assist the defenders of Poltava was most likely that Peter felt the time for a major confrontation was close. However, even following the information about Charles's injury and inability to lead the Swedish Army, Peter hesitated. He followed his commanders' advice to bring the main army across the Vorskla River, but insisted that any major confrontation with the Swedes should be avoided. On June 23, five days before Poltava, the Swedish Army assumed battle formations in the field in front of the huge fortified Russian camp. Peter, however, declined the invitation to bring his far superior army out to confront the enemy.

In a letter to his wife the day before the battle at Poltava, Menshikov advised that he felt very comfortable with the Russian defensive positions, that he did not expect the Swedes to attack, and that the Russian Army hoped shortly to relieve Poltava.[28] There was no suggestion that the Russian command hoped to pursue and defeat the Swedish Army. It appears that Menshikov might have been happy enough just to see the Swedes leave.

During the battle of Poltava, at a time when a third of the Swedish infantry was already lost, Menshikov suggested to Peter that he bring the Russian infantry out from the fortified camp onto the field to take on the Swedes. Peter declined. The major part of the Swedish Army had then passed through the outer Russian defensive system and had begun marching back and forth on the field in front of the Russian camp. Two hours later, with the Swedish Army still out on the field and with Rehnskjöld unable to decide what to do next, Peter finally took action. He brought out the Russian infantry, then four times the size of the enemy and supported by one hundred guns, as compared to four Swedish guns.

As a side note, Poltava was an absurdity that should never have happened. It was the result of Charles's insistence on having a decisive battle with Peter regardless of the odds. To explain how it came about, a conversation between Charles and Peter might have gone this way:

> **Charles.** Hi, Peter, I think we really should have this issue decided. I suggest our two armies meet on the field tomorrow in front of your fortified camp. I know you are comfortable there, but if you come out and meet us, we will have only half the number of infantry troops you have, and only two-thirds the size of your cavalry, and our artillery is only one-third of yours. But I think

we could have a fine and fair fight and settle everything.

Peter. No.

Charles. Oh, you don't like that. Then I have another proposal. You stay in your fortified camp, with all the redoubts in front to prevent hostile advances. We will come and attack your camp, still with only half or less your infantry force, although I know in these situations the attacking force should be at least twice the size of the defenders. And we will bring only four cannons, although I know you have about one hundred. And our gunpowder is so bad out musketeers can hardly get the bullet out of the musket. In addition, as you know, I was hit by one of your damn musket shots a few days ago, so I cannot lead my army, and my two chief commanders cannot get along, so you can be sure we will have a lot of confusion and mishaps.

Peter. Yes.

Charles. So you like that better. Okay, that's a deal.

GERMAN INVASION OF THE SOVIET UNION

Background and Planning

Germany in 1932

The enormous development in almost all aspects of society, industry, commerce, labor, and, of course, the military during the period 1812 to 1940 makes it desirable to provide more details about some areas and individuals of particular relevance to this work, during the period ten to fifteen years preceding World War II. Like literally all developed countries, Germany was hit hard by the 1930s depression. Problems in the Weimar Republic had started earlier than in most countries because it suffered under terms of the 1918 Versailles peace treaty, which presented almost insurmountable problems. The German economy was weak and the debt obligations, primarily to Britain and France, caused a strong downward pressure. When the worldwide depression hit, the Weimar leaders simply could not find an effective response. Since this was a time when currencies were tied to gold, the options available to stimulate an economy that was heading into depression were very limited. It is unlikely that Hitler's Nazi Party would have grown so dramatically between the 1928 and 1932 elections if Germany's economic decline had not been so steep. In 1928 German unemployment was 8.6 percent. In 1932 it was 33 percent. In the 1928 election, 1 percent of the votes went to the Nazi Party. In 1932 the Nazis received 37 percent and became the biggest party in the parliament.

The aging president Paul von Hindenburg resisted appointing Hitler to be chancellor (prime minister), but in the end, the combination of the terrible economic conditions in Germany and the Nazi Party's victory in the election forced Hindenburg's hand.[29]

Developments in Germany, 1932–39.

From a human rights perspective, the development in Germany from 1932 to 1939 could hardly have been worse. Economic policy was established by Hjalmar Schacht, who became head of the German Central Bank in 1933 and Hitler's minister of finance in 1934.[30] In many areas, economic improvements were exceptional. By 1939, unemployment had been reduced to the 6 to 7 percent level. There were some impressive projects, including the first divided highway system in the world.[31] Because of Hitler's priorities, the armament industry, in particular, experienced strong growth, but certain other sections of the economy, including consumer goods, fell behind.

Chancellor Adolf Hitler

Adolf Hitler was born in 1889 in Braunau-am-Inn in Austria, then part of the Austrian-Hungarian Empire. His family moved in 1906 to Lambach, Bavaria, where Hitler got his education. He left school at sixteen without a degree and moved to Vienna, where he tried to become an artist. In 1907–08 he submitted his watercolor paintings to the Vienna Academy of Fine Art, but they were rejected. After the second rejection, Hitler run out of money and had to live in homeless shelters or hostels. In 1913, he inherited some money when his father died, and moved to Munich. When World War I started in 1914, he joined the German Army, although an Austrian citizen.[32] During the war, he was twice awarded medals for bravery, the second time resulting from the recommendation of a Jewish officer. Through his demagogic oratory, he became politically successful as head of the National Socialist Workers Party (NSWP), which he created. As chancellor, Hitler quickly assumed dictatorial powers, although he lacked significant education regarding administrative or military matters. He ruled Germany until his death by suicide on April 30, 1945.

The Versailles Treaty greatly restricted Germany's military. The country could have no air force, the Army could not exceed one hundred thousand men, and no sophisticated military equipment could be manufactured in or imported to Germany. Even during the early days of the Weimar Republic, military and political organizations started violating terms of the treaty. One example is a secret arrangement, begun in 1923 with the Soviet Union, under which future German military pilots were trained in the Russian city of Lipetsk. This training went on until 1933, when Hitler renounced the Versailles Treaty. From then on, manufacturing in Germany was largely concentrated on the production of military equipment, including tanks, aircraft, and submarines.

The German Air Force was officially created in 1935. In the Spanish Civil War, German pilots gained opportunities to improve their skills at the same time as new German airplane designs could be tested.[33] When World War II broke out in September 1939, Germany had an Air Force with pilots far better trained and aircraft more effective and advanced than any other country in the world.

Developments in Military Doctrines, 1918 to 1939

In the two decades between the two World Wars, the art of warfare and the tools employed to conduct it probably changed more than in any similar period in history. This was particularly true for military aircraft and various armored and motorized vehicles. Airplanes and tanks had been introduced during World War I, but the Fokkers and Sopwith Camels employed during that war bore little resemblance to the Messerschmitts and Spitfires that appeared early in World War II. The same holds true for the types of tanks used in the two wars. While some German tanks in 1939 were so outdated as to be nearly obsolescent, they were still far more advanced than anything used twenty years earlier.

These changes had a profound impact on military doctrines and strategy. All the major countries struggled with these issues in different ways and with different results, particularly during the ten-year period leading up to World War II. The development and use of these new tools had to take into account the experiences of World War I. The French military planners had concluded that frontal attacks against fortified positions were almost suicidal. They decided that a solidly fortified border was the best defense. The Maginot Line was built along its German border from Switzerland to Belgium. Senior French commanders appear to have given little thought to how the Air Force and such armored forces, as had been introduced, should be employed. The young Charles de Gaulle was an exception. In 1934, he published a book called *The Army of the Future*. In it he predicted that tanks and other armored vehicles would be of paramount importance in any future war. He suggested that these weapons should be concentrated in separate units served by specially trained soldiers. The book was mostly ignored in France, but it received considerable attention in Germany.[34]

In the United Kingdom, the interest in the use of tanks was minimal among the senior levels of its military. However, Captain Liddell Hart, Major General J. F. C. Fuller, and a few other military historians had started in the late 1920s developing theories about how the new weapons might be employed in a future war. Their writings, like that of de Gaulle, received little attention in their home country, but they were studied with interest in some other countries. A number of young officers in the emerging German Army tried to inform themselves about the new weapons. General Heinz Guderian, one of Germany's most successful armored commanders in World War II, was among these early students of tanks and motorized troops. He presented his own thoughts, which were quite similar to those of Liddel Hart and de Gaulle, in a book published in 1938.[35] Senior military commanders in Germany, including Franz Halder, the head of the Army general staff, were skeptical of Guderian's ideas, but they caught the interest of Hitler. As a result, the theories of Guderian and his followers became the basis for the employment of armored forces in the German Army.

Separate armored divisions were created, consisting of one or two tank regiments and two or three regiments of motorized infantry. These divisions would also be supported by aircraft used for recognizance purposes but also capable of attacking enemy forces. The German armored forces played a decisive role in Germany's rapid defeat of the French and British forces in 1940. The French were not without tanks, and their tanks were almost as numerous, and some were as good or better than Germany's. However,

---

General Heinz Guderian

Heinz Guderian was born in 1888 to a Prussian military family in Kulm, Germany. As a young officer, he served in his father's regiment. He was ambitious and serious and studied both foreign languages and the newest technical developments like the use of radio communications. He stayed in the military after World War I and took an interest in the development of tanks and mobile warfare. In 1939, Guderian was appointed head of an armored corps, which contributed greatly to the victory in France in 1940. Guderian and his fellow tank commanders played a crucial role in the early victories of Barbarossa in 1941. Guderian was somewhat controversial because of a tendency to ignore orders from superiors. In 1940, General von Kleist wanted to fire Guderian for continuing his advance toward the English Channel despite orders to the contrary. Von Rundstedt saved him that time, but in December 1941, Hitler did fire him for retreating in violation of orders. However, following the Stalingrad defeat, Guderian was recalled to accelerate the development of the German mobile forces. He died in 1954.

the French did not know how to use them effectively. Their tanks were just positioned here and there among the infantry battalions and often ended up being almost useless.[36]

Some senior commanders in the Soviet Union started looking into the use of tanks in the late 1920s. Probably the most capable and talented of this group was Marshal Mikhail Tukhachevsky. He played a key role in developing mechanized forces in the Soviet Army as early as 1930. For several years, he held the second-ranking position in the Soviet military behind Voroshilov. Tukhachevsky prepared detailed regulations for the use of mechanized forces in the Soviet Army, which were issued in 1932 and 1936.[37] Largely thanks to Tukhachevsky, the development of tanks had produced good results by 1941. Unfortunately for the Soviet state, Stalin's paranoia and fears caused him to target his best commanders for his purges. Stalin was considering eliminating Tukhachevsky in 1930, but lacked support. In 1937, he found it. Tukhachevsky had played a crucial role in developing the new weapons. At Tukhachevsky's mock trial, the cavalry commander, Marshal Semyon Budyonny, testified that Tukhachevsky's advocacy of tanks and motorized troops was evidence in itself of treacherous intent.[38]

Stalin's elimination of many of the best Soviet military talents undoubtedly provided the Germans an important window of opportunity to destroy the Soviet armies before the surviving Soviet commanders had learned how to use their most important weapons.[39] Fortunately for the Germans, Budyonny, one of only two Soviet marshals to survive Stalin's persecutions, and not Tukhachevsky, was commander of the Soviet forces in the Ukraine in 1941.[40]

Germany's Military in September 1939

By September 1939, Germany had spent nearly six years building up its military forces.[41] In preparation for its invasion of Poland and war with the Western democracies, the Hitler regime entered into a treaty with the Soviet Union, the Nonaggression Pact of August 23, 1939. This pact provided that neither party would take military action against the other for a period of ten years. On September 1,

1939, Germany invaded Poland, prompting Britain and France to declare war against Germany. By then the German military included ten armored divisions, each consisting of two tank regiments of 150 tanks. In addition, two regiments of motorized infantry were part of each division. Compared to what the Germans would eventually face when encountering the Soviet Army, the German tanks were not very impressive.

The armored divisions that invaded France and the Low Countries in May 1940 consisted mostly of the Panzer I and Panzer II tanks, which were equipped with thin armor and only a twenty-millimeter cannon. Because the war started earlier than the industrial planners had expected, Panzer III and Panzer IV tanks, with much thicker armor and equipped with a fifty-seven-millimeter gun, were only available in small numbers. However, the German commanders knew how to use their tanks effectively. The German Air Force lent close support to the advancing tank regiments. The German Air Force in 1940 counted a total of about four thousand aircraft. The German industry was capable at that time of producing about seven hundred planes a month.

German Assessment of the Soviet Union

Hitler and many of his senior commanders greatly underestimated the Soviet military capability, much as Charles XII (but not Napoleon) had done in respect to Russia. In Hitler's view, Soviet vulnerability was proven by the weaknesses that the military demonstrated during the winter war of 1939–40 against Finland. The German military also assumed correctly that Stalin's purges weakened the Red Army. In fact, the lack of competent senior officers was a major cause of its poor performance in the Finnish war.

Reasons for War with the Soviet Union

In late spring of 1941, Germany occupied a place in Europe almost identical to the one Napoleon enjoyed when he invaded Russia in 1812. The German Army had ruthlessly eliminated all potential enemies on the continent, and the first successful parachute attack by the German Air Force in Crete was a dramatic demonstration of German military competence. As was the case for Napoleon, the only hostile power in sight was the British. The Soviet Union remained a powerful entity, but Germany had peace assured with the Soviets through the Nonaggression Pact, or so it would seem. In addition, on February 11, 1940, Germany and the Soviet Union had concluded a commercial agreement under which the Soviet Union would supply oil to Germany in return for advanced military equipment. The Soviets would also transmit to Germany products from third countries that might not want to deal directly with Germany.

Elements of friction had developed, however. In early June 1940, the Soviet Union invaded the Baltic States, and a few weeks later, forced Romania to surrender border territory. Hitler felt both of these acts went beyond the terms of the Nonaggression Pact. The move against Romania caused particular concern since it put Soviet forces closer to the Romanian oil fields. Romanian oil was crucial to meet Germany's need for energy. In response to the Soviet moves, Hitler ordered additional troops into the occupied parts of Poland.

Marshal Joseph Stalin

Joseph Stalin was born in Gori in Georgia in 1878. He had an intellectual bent, and as a teenager, submitted poems anonymously to his local newspaper. He took an early interest in Lenin's writings, and he joined the Bolshevik party. He was one of seven members of its first Politburo in 1917. Stalin impressed Lenin with his intellect and organizing talents. With Lenin's support, Stalin was elected general secretary of the party's Central Committee in 1922, a position he held for life. In the early years, he clashed frequently with Trotsky on political and strategic issues. A power struggle commenced in the party following Lenin's death. Stalin had an exceptional talent for political manipulation. As one observer has described it, he would gain the support of two Politburo members to advance in the party, then he would discard them and get in an alliance with a few other key persons and so on until he had gained absolute power.[42] His early insistence on industrialization of the Soviet Union proved critical in enabling the Soviet military to resist the German invasion in 1941. He had a better relationship with his senior commanders than Hitler, and despite his suspicious nature, Stalin was sometimes willing to listen to the advice of subordinates.[43] He died in 1953.

It has been suggested that Hitler, like Napoleon, believed an attack against the Soviet Union (Russia in Napoleon's case) would help defeat the British. In late 1940, Hitler had made peace proposals to the British, which some analysts described as surprisingly easy, considering the circumstances. But Winston Churchill and his government had rejected them. Hitler suspected that there were strong British efforts to make Stalin join the war against Germany. Accordingly, to Hitler it might have appeared that by eliminating the Soviet Union, he would solve the British problem as well.

Hitler's intense dislike of communism was unquestionably another motive. He explained to his commanders that unless the Bolshevik system was totally eliminated, communism would become an increasing threat to Western civilization. Hitler had violently suppressed the communists in Germany. Almost all their leaders were dead or in prison. There was also the German industry's need for oil and other industrial products. The commercial agreement entered into with the Soviets in February 1940 was helpful, but if the Soviet resources could be acquired, Germany would be in a far stronger position.

Finally, Hitler wanted more territory. The term *lebensraum* (living space) had become prominent during Hitler's attacks on Germany's neighbors in the years preceding World War II. Hitler supposedly believed that the Soviet Union could provide valuable land for German farmers once the current population was liquidated. The Ukraine was a tempting target.

Hitler received continuous intelligence from the German ambassador in Moscow and other sources that the Soviets were rearming. He appeared not to have taken these reports too seriously. Nonetheless, some of the German generals told Liddell Hart after the war that Hitler had advised them at various times in 1940–41 that the Soviets were preparing to attack Germany.[44] It is hardly likely that Hitler believed these claims himself. By late 1940, Hitler had decided to attack the Soviet Union. The attack was planned to start in early May 1941.[45]

Stalin's Reaction to the Threat

Long before the spring of 1941, Stalin was unquestionably concerned about what action Hitler might take. The Soviet troops' weak performance against Finland in the winter war of 1939–40 made an impression on Stalin, just as it had on the Germans. He concluded that the Soviet Union needed to delay a war with Germany as long as possible. So Stalin and his government faithfully complied with the Nonaggression Pact. The commercial agreement with Germany in January 1940 was another part of Stalin's policy of avoiding provocation and even providing help to his dangerous neighbor. The Soviets carried out the terms of these agreements until the German attack in 1941. Stalin even ordered Soviet troops not to be stationed too close to the German border to avoid possible provocation.

General Franz Halder

Franz Halder was born in 1884 in Wurzburg, Bavaria, to a family with long military traditions. He served as a staff officer during World War I and stayed in the military following the war. He gained a reputation as a skillful planner and became head of the Army General Staff in 1938, reporting to General von Brauchitsch. Halder and von Brauchitsch became concerned about Hitler's plans to invade Czechoslovakia in the fall of 1938 because they were convinced that Germany could not win a war against France and England. They organized a plot to overthrow and kill Hitler.[46] However, the Munich conference, plus Chamberlain's appeasement of Hitler, averted the Czech invasion. Halder aborted the coup. When the war started in September 1939, Halder and his deputy, von Paulus, became deeply involved in planning German attacks. Nonetheless, Halder was one of the few commanders who would question Hitler's proposals. By August 1942, the relationship had become close to unworkable, so Hitler fired him. Following the July 1944 assassination attempt on Hitler, the Gestapo investigated Halder and uncovered some of his earlier conspiracies. Halder was sent to a concentration camp from which he was rescued by American troops in May 1945. Halder had maintained a diary that proved very helpful to historians. He cooperated with the United States in various ways following the war and even received a service award. He died in 1972.

The German Strategic Plan

Planning for an invasion of the Soviet Union started in the summer of 1940. Three different groups prepared plans, which were submitted one after another to General Franz Halder, chief of the German Army General Staff, other top commanders, and, ultimately, to Hitler. All these plans were very ambitious. During the first thirty to forty days, the German armies were to destroy the main Soviet forces without having to advance beyond the Dnieper-Dvina rivers. In the second phase, the target was to capture Moscow. In the south, troops would reach the Volga River, and in the north, troops somehow would get all the way to Arkhangelsk—all accomplished by late fall 1941. In November 1940, Halder's deputy, General Friedrich von Paulus, was assigned to finalize the plans. He found the assumptions and conclusions of the initial plans, particularly those relating to the second phase, totally unrealistic and scaled them back drastically.

To test the assumptions of the modified plan, von Paulus arranged war games, which involved all the German key commanders. The enemy forces were estimated on the bases of army intelligence. Even the modified plan was extremely ambitious, considering the huge expanse of the enemy territory to be covered, the German commanders' lack of experience in operating under the conditions they would face in Russia, their incomplete and uncertain information concerning the Red Army's resources and the quite limited size of the German Army, especially its crucial mobile forces. In fact, following the war games, von Paulus concluded that the German forces were barely sufficient to accomplish the objectives. He recognized that the Soviets would be able to replace losses from their substantial reserve forces, even troops from the Far East, while German reserves were very limited. However, von Paulus was well aware of Hitler's extremely optimistic assessment of the relative German-Soviet strength. As a result, both von Paulus and Halder failed to express to Hitler some of their concerns about the feasibility of implementing the German plan.

Like the previous plans, the final plan aimed for decisive results during the first thirty to forty days. It contemplated a three-pronged advance. A northern force would go through the Baltic countries and seize Leningrad (now and previously St. Petersburg). A central force would advance through Minsk and Smolensk and eventually capture Moscow. Finally, a southern force would start at Brest Litovsk and proceed south of the Pripet Marshes toward Kiev and then on to Crimea and possibly the Caucasus. Like Napoleon, Hitler and his senior commanders, including General Walther von Brauchitsch, the supreme commander of the Army, assumed that the Soviets would put up a major fight close to the border. They believed that Stalin would feel it critical to defend the western part of the Soviet Union to protect its industrial capability. A principal objective was for the central and southern forces to destroy the opposing Soviet forces west of the Dnieper. In his comments on the Paulus-Halder plan, Hitler emphasized that the Soviet armies must not be permitted to retreat far into Russia or the Ukraine.[47]

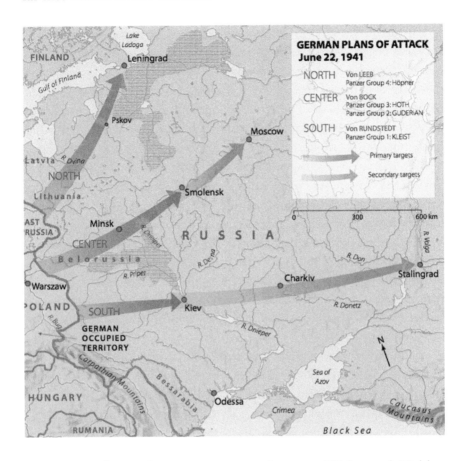

A significant disagreement arose between Hitler and Halder. Halder and von Brauchitsch felt strongly that conquering Moscow should be the ultimate goal. They believed that if the Soviet forces had not been completely defeated west of the Dnieper, conquering Moscow would be the key to victory. They assumed that if the Soviet forces lost Moscow, they would become so dejected and disorganized they could no longer resist. Hitler, however, insisted that the key objective should be the destruction of the Soviet Army and the Soviet industry, which he thought was located in the Ukraine and areas bordering on it. He considered Moscow of less importance. During the planning stage, Halder abstained from an open disagreement with Hitler. Instead, he decided to have the planned campaign proceed toward his targets, in particular Moscow, rather than pursue Hitler's objectives. Because Halder chose not to voice his objections openly, Hitler probably assumed that the matter was settled. However, the disagreement would arise again at a critical point during the actual campaign. According to some of the senior German commanders, including General Guderian, Hitler's rejection of Halder's advice contributed greatly to Germany's failure to secure victory before the end of 1941.

On December 18, 1940, Hitler issued Directive No. 21. It read in part:

> "(Operation Barbarossa[48])
>
> The German Armed Forces must be prepared, even before concluding the war against England, to crush the Soviet Union in a rapid campaign."

The Invasion

Balkan Diversion

Hitler initially selected May 15, 1941, as the start of Operation Barbarossa. However, complications interfered. On October 28, 1940, Mussolini began an invasion of Greece by forces stationed in Albania. The operation turned into a disaster for the Italians as the Greeks launched a counteroffensive that drove the Italians back into Albania. By early 1941, Greek forces controlled 25 percent of that country.

The matter irritated Hitler greatly. His Axis partner had not consulted him in advance about the Greek campaign. Before launching Barbarossa, Hitler wanted to safeguard his southern flank. He had been successful in getting assurances of cooperation from Hungary, Romania, and Bulgaria. Greece presented a problem, however. In view of the war with Italy, the Greek government was not inclined to cooperate with Germany. In addition, Greece had received assurances of help from the British. This made Hitler feel that despite possible delays of Barbarossa, the Greek conflict had to be settled. On April 7, 1941, German and Bulgarian troops crossed the border into Greece from Bulgaria. The British assistance was much too limited to have any significant impact on the outcome. On April 28, Greek resistance terminated, and an armistice was concluded with Germany and Italy. So in less than two weeks, the Germans won a war that Italy had fought unsuccessfully for five months.

However, another complication arose about the time the Germans and their Bulgarian allies launched the Greek campaign. A sudden coup in Yugoslavia overthrew its pro-German government. Hitler found it necessary to intervene. Along with Hungarian allies, the Germans entered Yugoslavia on April 7, 1941. By April 17, a new pro-German government had been installed in Belgrade.

These events delayed Barbarossa from May 15 to June 22, 1941—an amazingly short delay, considering the two very significant problems with which the German military had to deal. Nonetheless, there has been some suggestion that even this delay of barely five weeks may have been fatal to the German objectives. The justification for this argument is that the delay caused the final assault on Moscow to take place under winter conditions. The German troops were not equipped for that type of warfare.

Military Forces in June 1941

The Army that Germany engaged for Barbarossa consisted of 116 infantry and 19 armored divisions, with 3,600 tanks and motorized infantry, and one cavalry division. There were also about seventy-five reserve divisions, which were not as well trained. Many of these were tied up in areas occupied by Germany in Western Europe and Scandinavia. About seventy thousand pieces of artillery were assigned to the Barbarossa force. Almost 50 percent of the German tanks were of a light model with such thin armor (twenty millimeters) and light armament that they were hardly suitable for a campaign like Barbarossa.

Each armored division, in addition to tanks, included about nineteen thousand motorized infantry. Heavy trucks were supposed to enable the infantry to move fast enough to support the tank force and to break through enemy lines. Ideally, even the regular infantry, by far the biggest part of the army, should have had access to trucks to make sure that contact could be maintained between the fast-moving armored divisions and the rest of the troops. However, the German Army simply did not have enough trucks. In finalizing the plans for Barbarossa, Halder found the deficiency so drastic that he requisitioned 750,000 horses and wagons to fill the gap. Not surprisingly, the lack of adequate transportation equipment would hamper the advancing German forces the farther they advanced into Russia.

Luftwaffe had an important part to play in the campaign. Close air support of the advancing mobile forces was considered crucial for success. However, Luftwaffe had suffered great losses in the unsuccessful attempt to defeat the British RAF in 1940. Barbarossa was allocated fewer than three thousand aircraft, a quite modest number considering the huge space and aggressive objectives of the campaign. In addition, in June 1941, more than 20 percent of the airplanes allocated were out of service for maintenance or repair. The demands of Barbarossa substantially reduced Luftwaffe's operations against England.

When the Germans attacked, the portion of the Red Army stationed in the western part of the Soviet Union consisted of around ninety infantry divisions, fifty-four armored divisions, and seven cavalry divisions. The Germans knew that the Red Army probably had a substantial number of tanks. Field Marshal Wilhelm Keitel, who served in effect as Hitler's minister of war, estimated the Soviet armored force to number thirty-five divisions of tanks. Keitel assured the German generals that the quality of the Red Army's tank force was far inferior to that of the German, both in respect to the commanders and crews of the tanks and the tanks themselves. Concerning the former, Keitel's assessment was essentially correct, but it was significantly wrong in respect to the quality of the tanks.

In 1941, the Soviet Army may have had as many as twenty thousand tanks, but most were very old, light tanks with no more than fifteen- to twenty-millimeter armor. Like the older German tanks, they were hardly adequate for the upcoming battle. In addition, their commanders and crews were poorly trained. However, the Soviet industry had developed much improved tanks, the KV-1 and the T-34. In June 1941, they were far superior to anything available in the German Army. They had much thicker armor and a 7.5 centimeter gun (at that time, they were the only tanks in any army with such heavy guns; the new German Mark III and Mark IV tanks had a 5.7 centimeter gun). Tanks with these caliber guns could destroy the best German tanks from a distance of two thousand meters while the German tanks had to be within five hundred meters of a T-34 to be effective. It would not be until the middle of 1943 that the Germans introduced tanks of this quality. When Barbarossa was launched, the Soviets had about 1,500 KV-1 or T-34 tanks in service. Fortunately for the Germans, their crews were no better trained than the rest of the Soviet tank force.

Even in respect to artillery, the Red Army enjoyed a substantial superiority as compared to the German forces. According to some estimates, the Red Army had as many as thirty-five thousand pieces of artillery in 1941.

The Soviet Union had been developing its Air Force since the late 1920s and all through the 1930s. When Barbarossa started, the portion of the Soviet Air Force allocated to assist in the immediate defense was at least three times bigger than Luftwaffe's forces. The Soviet airplanes were somewhat inferior to those of the Germans, but the biggest problem was the lack of training and experience of the Soviet pilots and their commanders. The Soviet Air Force, like other parts of the Soviet military, had suffered greatly as a result of Stalin's purges. These weaknesses helped Luftwaffe destroy thousands of Soviet planes within the first couple of weeks of Barbarossa, with very minor German losses. Most of the Soviet aircraft were destroyed on the ground.

The Start of Barbarossa

In the early morning of June 22, 1941, German soldiers invaded the Soviet Union. The advance followed fairly closely the Halder/Paulus plan, with the attacking German forces divided into three separate groups. Field Marshal Ritter von Leeb commanded Army Group North. His army consisted of 26 infantry divisions, five armored divisions, about five hundred thousand soldiers and one thousand tanks. General Erich Hoepner was the tank commander. The advance started from East Prussia and proceeded through the Baltic countries with the goal of conquering Leningrad.

Army Group Center, under Field Marshal Fedor von Bock, crossed the Niemen River fairly close to where Napoleon's main force had crossed in 1812. Von Bock's group consisted of about fifty infantry divisions and ten armored divisions, organized in two Panzer groups, commanded by Generals Guderian and Hoth. The armored forces, just under two hundred thousand soldiers and about two thousand tanks, amounted to only 16 to 17 percent of von Bock's total force. Nonetheless, the Germans believed that these troops were the key to a fast and overwhelming victory. That was the conventional wisdom from the operations against the French and the British in 1940. Von Bock was aiming for Minsk in Belarus and then Smolensk in Russia. Eventually, Moscow

Marshal Semyon Timoshenko

Semyon Timoshenko was born in a small Ukrainian town in 1895. He was drafted and served in the cavalry during World War I. Following the Communist revolution, he got command of a cavalry regiment in the Red Army. During that war, he happened to meet with Stalin, in charge of the defense of Stalingrad (at that time known as Tsaritsyn). This early connection to Stalin created a route for his military career. He advanced rapidly and became valuable to Stalin as a dependable ally during the purges. By 1939, Timoshenko had become commissar of defense. Although inclined toward classical warfare, Timoshenko advocated modernizing the Army including developing the armored forces. When the Germans attacked in 1941, Timoshenko was in charge of the Central Front facing von Bock's Army Group Center. Subsequently, Timoshenko held various major positions until the end of the war in 1945. He died in 1970.

might become a target. Marshal Semyon Timoshenko commanded the troops opposing von Bock's force. His infantry force was about the same size as that of the attacking Germans. Timoshenko possessed nearly three thousand tanks, but for the most part they were drastically out of date. Nonetheless, they included perhaps as many as five hundred to six hundred of the highly effective T-34 model.

The third attacking army, Army Group South, was commanded by Field Marshal Gerd von Rundstedt. His force was almost identical in size to von Leeb's army. However, his armored force, commanded by General Paul Ludwig von Kleist, was below normal strength because von Kleist's Panzer divisions had been employed in the Greek campaign. The tight timetable between that project and Barbarossa had not permitted maintenance and repair of damaged tanks. At the start of Barbarossa, von Kleist's total armored force was just 650 tanks. Von Rundstedt's group started in the Brest-Litovsk area and advanced south of the Pripet Marshes aiming for Kiev and eventually the Donetsk region of the Ukraine. Von Rundstedt's troops faced a Soviet Army commanded by Marshal Semyon Budyonny. It amounted to about nine hundred thousand men, including an armored force of up to five thousand tanks.

The German plan was quite similar to that of Napoleon's 130 years earlier. In a statement of strategy in late fall of 1940, Hitler announced that the German Army was to engage the Soviet forces quickly and prevent them from retreating deep into Russia. The basic objective was to essentially eliminate the Soviet Army within four weeks and without German forces having to advance east of the Dnieper River. Napoleon had expected to complete his campaign successfully within three weeks. The end results were not that different.

Von Bock's Advance

The advance of von Bock's group was initially spectacular. His forces reached Minsk, 350 kilometers from the Niemen River, in just nine days. However, despite their fast advance, the Germans succeeded in encircling and capturing only a modest number of Soviet troops close to the border. When the German forces reached Minsk, a significant number of prisoners were captured.[49]

To carry out their encircling maneuvers, the Germans depended initially on their armored divisions. During the follow-up and completion of the operation, strong support by the German infantry was needed. However, the German transportation capability was not good enough to move the infantry at a speed even close to that of the armored troops. The Germans did not have enough heavy trucks, nor were they equipped with tracks. As a result, when the weather got wet, the trucks got stuck in the mud. This weak transportation capability became an increasing problem. While the tanks divisions were operated with great efficiency, they still needed help from the infantry to close the pockets and hold off Soviet counterattacks.

As the German troops approached the Smolensk area, almost five hundred kilometers from their starting point, Guderian and Hoth's Panzer groups raced ahead to close a pocket, which, the German believed, might capture as many as six hundred thousand enemy troops. This operation developed into an extremely tough and quite lengthy battle. Marshal Timoshenko was able to bring in fresh troops to attack the advanced German positions.

The slow progress of the German infantry forced Guderian's and Hoth's divisions to defend their advanced positions alone. They fought desperately from the middle of July until early August, barely holding on to their gains and without succeeding in closing the Smolensk pocket. The partially encircled Soviet forces kept slipping out, and Timoshenko's fresh troops launched energetic counterattacks to force a German retreat. The battle was undecided for several weeks and pushed the endurance of the advancing German force close to the breaking point.

Finally, on August 6, von Bock was able to announce that the pocket had been closed, resulting in the capture of as many as three hundred thousand Soviet troops. However, about 50 percent of the originally "caught" Soviet forces escaped. While a significant German success, the Smolensk operation was not a decisive victory, and it came at a heavy cost for the Germans, especially to their crucial armored forces. Almost 30 percent of Guderian's and Hoth's tanks were lost, and 25 percent required repair before being again put in action.[50]

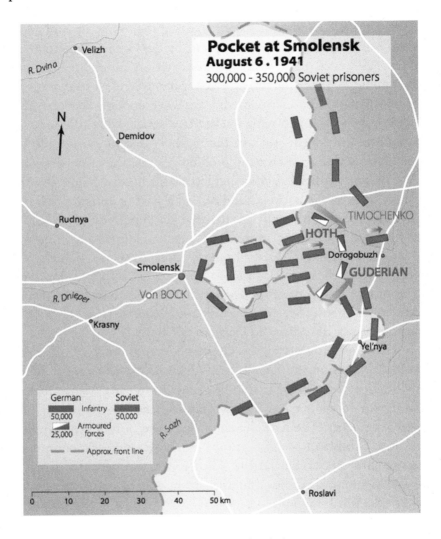

In late July 1941, Hitler approached the Japanese government about the desirability of Japan entering the war.[51]

The Pocket at Kiev

The disagreement between Hitler and Halder, which first surfaced in the fall of 1940, emerged full blown following the Smolensk battle. Halder, von Bock, and von Brauchitsch now wanted all forces of Army Group Center allocated to an attack against Moscow. Hitler, however, considered Moscow less important than defeating the Soviet Army and conquering or destroying its industry. Before this argument was settled, Hitler agreed with von Brauchitsch to allow a period of rest for the troops and for service and replacement of equipment. This also enabled the senior commanders, including Guderian, to present their arguments to Hitler in favor of the Moscow option. Still, Hitler insisted on the Kiev-first approach. Hitler had noted that the rapid advance of von Rundstedt's forces in the Ukraine had created an opportunity to encircle a large Soviet force in the Kiev area.

Field Marshal Gerd Von Rundstedt

Gerd von Rundstedt was born in 1875 to a Prussian family with a long military tradition. He served as a staff officer during World War I and remained in the military following that war. He retired as a general in 1938, but was recalled when World War II started and commanded one of the two major groups that invaded Poland and France. During Barbarossa, von Rundstedt commanded Army Group South advancing toward Kiev. Despite the successful encirclement of a huge Soviet force at Kiev, von Rundstedt was fired by Hitler in December 1941 for disregarding Hitler's directions. He was recalled and commanded the German forces defending against the 1944 allied invasion in Normandy. Von Rundstedt repeatedly rejected invitations to join conspiracies against Hitler, but never reported them. Eisenhower considered him the most capable of the German generals. He died in 1953.

To assist von Rundstedt in exploiting this situation, General von Kluge's Fourth Army, including Guderian's Panzer group, was temporarily transferred from Army Group Center to von Rundstedt's Army Group South. The plan was for von Kleist's armored forces, coming from the south, to connect east of Kiev with Guderian's Panzer divisions advancing from the north. This operation was successfully completed, and the two armored groups closed a huge pocket on September 3. They encircled a Russian force consisting of most of the Soviet South Western Front. Marshal Zhukov had warned

Stalin that the troops of this front at and around Kiev were in danger of encirclement, but Stalin would not listen. As at Smolensk, the Russian soldiers fought hard, but eventually a very large number surrendered. However, this remarkable victory was not completed until September 10. In the meantime, von Bock's Group Center had been standing more or less still.

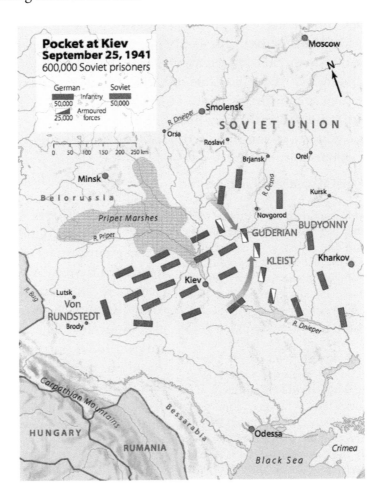

The Drive on Moscow

After the intensive battle in the Smolensk area, the period of time designated for the troops' rest and service of their equipment, coupled with the diversion of a significant portion of von Bock's troops to von Rundstedt's group, inevitably delayed by four or five weeks any further action by Army Group Center. This delay was made worse by Hitler's failure to decide the next step. Not until October 2 was von Bock authorized to begin the advance toward Moscow. Some historians feel Hitler wasted two months—and from a weather point of view, two good months—before launching what was hoped to be the final attack.

At this point in early October, von Kluge and several other commanders questioned whether it was still possible to successfully execute such an ambitious advance. In the Army's progress since June, all had experienced the tremendous difficulties in moving infantry fast enough on the poor Russian roads. The big trucks were getting stuck in the mud, and the infantry was left far behind the tank formations. Bringing up sufficient supplies had been equally difficult. With winter approaching, these problems would, of course, get even worse.

The generals were told that Hitler had information that the Soviet defense was about to collapse. So despite their concerns, the drive to take Moscow—named Operation Typhoon—was ordered to start. Von Kluge's Fourth Army had the center position. The Fourth Army was supported by the Ninth Army and Hoth's Panzer Group 3 in the north and by the Second Army and Hoepner's Panzer Group 4 on the southern flank. In addition, Guderian's Second Panzer Group was on its way back from its Kiev campaign to join the attack. In total, Operation Typhoon involved up to one million soldiers, 1,500 tanks, and 14,000 pieces of artillery. Luftwaffe was providing support but had lost almost 2,000 aircraft since June 22. It had only 600 aircraft available for Typhoon.

The defending Soviet forces numbered more than 1,200,000 troops from three different fronts, about 1,000 tanks and around 10,000 artillery pieces. They had the support of about 1,000 aircraft. A large proportion of the Soviet armies were concentrated around Vyazma and Bryansk, located between Smolensk and Moscow. The Soviet commanders had not expected an offensive so late in the year. As a result, by October 10, the German Panzer groups had succeeded in encircling the defenders in both Vyazma and Bryansk. While a significant number of Soviet troops managed to sneak out of the pocket, as many as 350,000 may have ended up as prisoners.

The Soviet losses at Vyazma and Bryansk amounted to about one-third of the forces defending Moscow. Nonetheless, the German advance from Vyazma was slow. The roads were as terrible as the German commanders had feared, and even the tanks had a hard time in the mud. Hitler wanted the troops in all three areas, Army Groups North and South as well as Center, to maintain attacks. Following the latest German victory at Vyazma, he assumed that the Soviet Army could not recover. The commanders in the field were getting increasingly dubious, however. Von Leeb in the north and von Rundstedt near Crimea advised that their troops were in no condition for another offensive. In addition, supplies were lacking. Von Bock's number 2, von Kluge, was doubtful about the potential for further advance, despite the success at Vyazma. The troops involved in Typhoon suffered increasingly from the Russian winter, which had started in the middle of October. By early November, snow was getting deep, and temperatures dropped to -25 degrees Celsius or lower.

On November 15, Halder arranged a meeting at Orso, south of Moscow, with representatives of all three groups to get a better picture of the attitude of the field commanders. The representatives of Group North, von Leap, and Group South, von Rundstedt, both responded in the negative concerning any farther advance until spring 1942 at the earliest. Von Bock's Group Center, alone, favored a last attempt to advance. So von Kluge agreed to have the Fourth Army move ahead supported by the three Panzer groups. However, the weather got no better and the extreme cold continued, making it difficult for even the tanks and other weapons to function. In addition, the German formations faced increasing resistance from Soviet forces reinforced by fresh reserves.

In recollections after the war, General Günther Blumentritt, who served as chief of staff of von Kluge's army, described the attitude and feelings of the German commanders at this stage of the advance. According to Blumentritt, von Kluge and most of his senior assistants had little faith that they could reach Moscow. Many of them recalled

Napoleon's disastrous 1812 campaign. Blumentritt described how von Kluge studied Caulaincourt's account of Napoleon's campaign on an almost daily basis.[52] In late November, von Kluge brought the Fourth Army's advance to almost a complete halt to evaluate the situation with his staff.

After some day's hesitation, von Kluge resumed the offensive. During von Kluge's slowdown, the Panzer Groups had continued to press ahead and reached positions much in front of the main attacking force. Unprepared for winter conditions, the German soldiers suffered greatly from the exceptional cold. Guderian thought his personnel losses excessive and complained to his superiors, von Bock, von Brauchitsch, and even Hitler, that he lost more soldiers to extreme cold than to enemy fire. Guderian wanted to stop the offensive and instead retreat to defensible positions. However, he was ordered by Hitler to press ahead and take Tula, a crucial location south of Moscow. He tried but failed. The weather was too bad, the defense too solid, and he had too few tanks left. Nevertheless, despite all difficulties, on December 2, units of Hoepner's Panzer group had advanced close enough to the goal to view the Kremlin.

The next day, Marshal Zhukov launched a massive counterattack. It quickly put the advanced German forces into serious peril. Following the war, von Kluge, Blumentritt, and other German commanders related that they had not expected so vigorous a counterattack nor such a large force. They maintained that about one hundred Soviet divisions had been involved, far more than what they had thought possible by a supposedly collapsing army.

Zhukov's forces may not have been quite that large, but he had received reinforcements of at least thirty Siberian divisions, which were reasonably well trained and equipped with T-34 tanks.[53] Zhukov pushed ahead to accomplish the type of encirclements that previously the Germans had done. Von Kluge and Blumentritt tried to convince Hitler to allow a withdrawal to a more defensible line but were denied. Hitler would permit no retreat. Several Panzer divisions in the most exposed positions were nearly surrounded. The main German forces fought furiously and managed to hang on to villages, towns, and other important areas. In mid-January, Hitler finally relented and permitted some divisions to retreat. This relieved the situation for the German troops, and an uneven front was eventually stabilized.

The Situation in Early 1942

Marshal Georgy Zhukov

Georgy Zhukov was born in 1896 to a poor peasant family west of Moscow. In 1915, he was drafted into the Army. He served as a noncommissioned officer in the Russian cavalry during World War I. Following the war, he joined the Red Army during the civil war and stayed in the Army following the end of this war in 1921. He gradually advanced during the in-between war years and was one of the few promising young commanders to escape Stalin's purges. In 1938, he was appointed head of Soviet forces in Mongolia trying to stop Japanese troops advancing into Soviet territory. In a counteroffensive, he pioneered the use of tanks and aircraft and succeeded in encircling and defeating the principal Japanese force. When the Germans launched Barbarossa, Zhukov was head of the Soviet General Staff. As such, he unsuccessfully advised against counteroffensives in the early stages to avoid encirclements. After an argument with Stalin in August 1941 over the strategy at Kiev, Zhukov resigned as head of the General Staff. Stalin put him in charge of reserve forces, but when the situation on the Moscow front became critical, he was put in operational command of all forces defending Moscow. Subsequently, he was in charge of Soviet troops at Stalingrad and at Kursk. He has been considered by many, including some of the senior German generals, the most successful top commander in World War II. He died in 1974.

Despite their recent problems, in early 1942, the Germans could look back on gains since the beginning of Barbarossa that were nearly unprecedented in scope. All three attacking Army groups had made tremendous territorial advances. Around 1,500,000 enemy soldiers were prisoners, and about as many were killed or injured. Thousands of tanks and a large part of the Soviet Air Force had been destroyed. Nonetheless, the campaign's two major objectives had not been achieved. As demonstrated by Zhukov's counteroffensive, the Soviet Army was far from destroyed. In fact, despite the heavy losses suffered by the Soviet Army during the period from June 22 to December 31, it still had as many soldiers as when the war started. This was very much the result of Stalin's efforts, started many years back, to have the army build up reserve forces in the millions. Of course, most of these forces were not as well trained as the troops lost. However, many officers, and especially the senior commanders, had gained experience and were becoming more capable. This was of particular importance in handling the growing Soviet Panzer force.

The German armies also had incurred great losses, amounting to at least eight hundred thousand men, around 50 percent of the tank force and about as big a percentage of Luftwaffe's resources.

Regarding the Soviet industry, the Germans had conquered important industrial areas in the western Soviet Union. However, Stalin had begun relocating major segments of the country's industries to areas east of the Ural Mountain even before the Germans attacked. These moves succeeded: in 1942, the Soviet produced four times as many tanks as the Germans (twenty-four thousand as compared to six thousand), and the Soviet tanks were mostly T-34s—tanks that, despite certain engine weaknesses, were overall superior to any tank model used or produced by the Germans at that time. In 1942, the Soviet production of aircraft exceeded that of the Germans, twenty-five thousand to fifteen thousand.

A big problem for the Germans was that their military industry was involved in a two-front war as soon as Barbarossa was launched. The Battle of the Atlantic had gone on since World War II started. It had gradually intensified, and after 1940, the Germans came to use submarines as their principal weapons. In September 1939, the Germans had only around fifty submarines, but during the next five years, they produced another 1,200, far more than any other country. The United States was a distant second with 250 submarines. That was the result of Hitler's decree that the Navy, and in particular submarines, would have top priority for German industrial resources. Next came the Air Force, followed by the Army in third place.

The concentration on submarines made some sense because in 1942, the Germans were coming close to winning the Battle of the Atlantic. Until the United States got involved, the British simply did not have enough vessels to combat Germany's growing submarine fleet. The number of commercial ships sunk made it almost impossible to maintain adequate supplies for the British Isles.[54] More help from the United States was badly needed. Its entry into the war marked a turning point. However, many months were still required before the joint efforts of the British, the Canadians, and the Americans could control Hitler's submarines. A tremendous number of antisubmarine vessels of all kinds, as well as escort carriers and long-distance aircraft capable of discovering and destroying submarines, were built. Gradually, this force changed the balance in the Atlantic. By mid-1943, the German submarines no longer constituted a major threat to British supplies. The allied success in the Battle of the Atlantic also resulted in drastically reduced losses in the British and American convoys passing by the coast of Norway and providing crucial support for the Soviet Union.

Hitler's allocation of industrial resources was probably right considering Germany's overall objectives in the war. However, it reduced the Germans' ability to produce aircraft, tanks, artillery, heavy trucks, and other products needed by the land forces. Such production was further hampered by shortages of raw materials. As a result, from 1942 through the end of the war, the relative strength of armored vehicles and other industrial products used in the war gradually shifted in favor of the Soviet Union. Manpower, too, became an increasing problem for the Germans after heavy losses in the Barbarossa campaign. Beginning in 1942, it had become difficult to maintain the numerical strength of the armies. More and more, the Germans had to depend on troops from its allies, the Romanians, Hungarians, Bulgarians, and Italians.

There is no question that, like Napoleon's 1812 campaign, Barbarossa's best chance for success was during the early months. By December 1941, was it still possible for Germany to win? Stahel concluded that by then the chances were very poor. In fact, he argues that already following the battle of Smolensk, which essentially ended in early August 1941, it was clear that Barbarossa would fail.

Stahel provides significant evidence in support of his conclusions.[55] But was the issue really decided so soon, less than two months following the launch of Barbarossa?

Many of the senior German commanders, including von Bock, Halder, and von Brauchitsch, felt Moscow would have been conquered if Hitler had not insisted on diverting troops from Army Group Center to Army Group South and even to Army Group North. Unlike Hitler, they thought that Moscow was the decisive target, and that if it fell, Soviet resistance would collapse. They were probably correct that Moscow might have been taken if the advance from the Smolensk area had started a month earlier—in early September instead of early October. However, their second conclusion is questionable. Zhukov's powerful counteroffensive, starting on December 4, demonstrated that the Soviet Army was far from defeated. In addition, reallocation of Guderian's Panzer group and other troops from Army Group Center to von Rundstedt's group resulted in the almost total destruction of Budyonny's Southern Front. Without this German victory, Budyonny's troops could have become a serious threat to the southern flank of German forces advancing toward Moscow.

Even if early August 1941 appeared too early to write off the German potential, what was the situation in early 1942? Observers around Europe, not the least in neutral Sweden, fully expected a resumption of the German offensive, once conditions improved in the spring of 1942. The failure of the German troops to conquer Moscow and their subsequent retreat were surprising. Yet the previous performance of the German military was so impressive that most people assumed that the campaign would end successfully, once the weather improved. In a letter to Roosevelt on March 7, 1942, Churchill wrote in part, "Everything portends an immense renewal of the German invasion of Russia in the spring..."[56]

Most of the senior German commanders felt quite differently. Field Marshals von Rundstedt and von Leeb, commanding two of the three German attacking groups, advised Hitler against any further offensive and instead suggested their troops be withdrawn to the German border. Von Brauchitsch and Halder also cautioned against further advance. Both von Rundstedt and von Leeb resigned because of tactical disagreements with Hitler. Von Brauchitsch was fired as commander in chief of the Army because of the Army's failure to accomplish the objectives of Barbarossa in 1941. The Army's star panzer general, Guderian, was also fired in early 1942 for withdrawing his forces in violation of Hitler's orders. Von Bock was temporarily relieved for ill health. So only Halder remained of the original senior team.

Halder and his senior advisors estimated that the Army would need an infusion of eight hundred thousand men to launch an offense in the spring of 1942. That size force was not readily available. A substantial number of men at work in industry would have to be called in. However, Albert Speer, minister of armament production, advised Hitler that he could not possibly spare any significant number of workers without jeopardizing war production. The problem was solved by reducing the number of battalions in each division from nine to seven. In addition, the number of soldiers in each company was reduced from around two hundred to one hundred.

Two new armored divisions were created during early 1942, again by reducing the number of tanks in each existing division. As a result, there was no increase in the number of tanks, but overall quality was improved. This was accomplished by the German production during 1941 of around 3,500 tanks. All were the more powerful Panzer III and Panzer IV, replacing the inferior Panzer I and II tanks.

The 1942 Offensive

In the spring of 1942, Hitler was in a difficult situation, rather similar to the one in which Napoleon found himself at Vitebsk in July 1812 and a few weeks later at Smolensk. Hitler's assault on the Soviet Union had produced some amazing victories and demonstrated the ability of the German generals, the endurance of the German soldiers, and, perhaps most importantly, the outstanding skill of the German panzer commanders. And still, the chief objectives of Barbarossa, the total defeat of the Soviet Army and the capture or destruction of the Soviet industry, had not been accomplished. In addition, what had been achieved had not come easily. The Soviet troops had fought much harder than expected, and the German casualties, although much lower than those of the enemy, were still huge.

Hitler's senior commanders were almost unanimous in cautioning against another big offensive in 1942. Their feeling was that the German resources, which were no bigger than in the spring of 1941 and actually were weaker in some areas, were not sufficient to accomplish in 1942 what Germany had been unable to do in 1941. But if the German forces were not to launch a new offensive, what should they do? To remain where they were, far deeper into Russia and the Ukraine than had been planned, was hardly acceptable. It also would be very costly. Big efforts would be required to supply the armies, the troops would continue to suffer casualties, and nothing would be gained. So if a new offensive was not appropriate, maybe the suggestions of von Rundstedt and von Leeb were right. Retreat back to the 1941 German border. Or perhaps there was still another option. Approach Stalin and suggest peace negotiations.

Hitler and his commanders had planned for Barbarossa to be a fast operation, resulting in the destruction of the Soviet military forces and its industry in a few months without German troops advancing east of the Dnieper River. In early 1942, it was clear that neither the Soviet forces nor its industry had been destroyed, despite substantial German losses in personnel and material. Moreover, there was reason to question, as most of the senior German commanders did, whether a new German offensive in the spring or summer of 1942 could accomplish a decisive victory. So under those circumstances, why not get out of the whole operation?

A peace treaty, including withdrawal of German troops all the way to the Polish border, would have relieved tremendous pressure on the German military. It also would have opened the possibility for the German forces to move in other areas. The Middle East, in particular, would have been an opportunity. In early 1942, Rommel was planning attacks in North Africa, with Cairo as a possible goal. If significant forces could have been reallocated from the Russian front to Rommel, much could have been achieved. The oil fields in Iraq would have been a realistic target. Such an operation might have gained Germany the supply of oil it needed and made any additional efforts in Russia unnecessary.

There would, of course, have been the question whether Stalin would have been interested in peace at this time. He did allow Molotov to meet for peace talks with von Ribbentrop in Kirovograd in the Ukraine in June 1943.[57] At that time, following the Stalingrad victory, the Soviet Union was in a far stronger position than in the spring of 1942. Even though Zhukov's counteroffensive in December 1941 had eliminated the immediate German threat to Moscow, the German Army remained in positions from which new attacks could be launched. So Stalin might have been willing to explore a peace proposal in February or March of 1942.[58]

However, for Hitler, just as in the end for Napoleon at Vitebsk, such a decision was almost impossible. Proposing peace would inevitably be interpreted as an admission that Barbarossa had failed. Hitler could not face that. He acted like Napoleon in Vitebsk and Smolensk, and like Charles XII after Lesnaya and Baturin. Hitler could not accept the logical consequences of Barbarossa's less than complete success in 1941. He refused to take the steps that might have saved Germany, even at this stage of the war. Instead he plunged the country into a new, very complicated, ambitious, and eventually disastrous offensive.

It appears that Hitler had been looking for help in making a decision. Such help preferably should point in the direction he wanted. He knew this decision would be almost as fateful as the one that launched Barbarossa in the first place. He got the push he needed from his economists. They told him Germany could not long continue prosecuting the war without certain minerals and—most urgently—oil, all of which could be found in the Ukraine and the Caucasus. So with the help of Halder, plans for a new offensive were put together. The Army would advance all the way to the Caucasus and capture the oil fields in Maikop and Grozny. Then the forces would continue through the mountain chain to Baku on the Caspian Sea. If successful, the expectation was that this action would not only provide Germany with all needed oil, it might also cut off the Soviet oil supply.

Maikop, the closest oil center, was located about 1,200 kilometers from Kharkov, Ukraine, the location in the spring of 1942 of the First Panzer Army, selected to lead the German advance. Clearly, the new offensive plans entailed tremendous challenges. In 1941, supplying the fast advancing panzer forces had repeatedly presented problems that the Germans lacked adequate resources to solve. As much as Russian resistance, this had contributed to the slowdown of the German offensive and eventually to its complete halt. The new plans for the summer of 1942 contemplated advances more than three times farther into enemy territory than had Barbarossa. Considering the experiences in 1941, how were these challenges to be mastered in 1942?

In addition, even if the plans were totally successful, how would the benefits be secured? The plan did not aim to destroy either the Soviet military or its industrial capacity. The size of the Soviet military was bigger than in June 1941, and the Soviet industry was steadily improving, producing far more tanks and aircraft than Germany. If the 1942 campaign did give Germany control of the principal Soviet oil centers, how would the German forces be able to protect the shipping lines of the oil from the Caucasus to Germany? The distance from the closest oil centers to the major German industries was around three thousand kilometers, and a big portion of the transportation routes would be highly vulnerable to Soviet attacks.

There were few troops, either German or from Germany's allies, available to protect such routes. With the Soviet forces remaining undefeated and steadily increasing in strength, this task was clearly far beyond the capability of the German military. It seems likely that Hitler had given such concerns little thought. In his position, he could not afford negative possibilities to enter into his calculations. An example of Hitler's refusal to face realities occurred when Halder advised that German intelligence indicated that the Soviets in the spring of 1942 were producing seven hundred tanks a month. Hitler flatly dismissed this as an impossibility.

To carry out the new offensive, the German forces in Russia and the Ukraine had been reorganized into two new entities: Army Group A, including the Seventeenth Army and the First Panzer Army, both from Army Group South, commanded by General List, and Army Group B, the Sixth Army from Army Group Center and the Fourth Panzer Army from Army Group North. Von Bock, who had returned to active duty, was given Army Group B. Army Group A was to realize the objectives in the Caucasus. Army Group B was to advance in the direction of Stalingrad, located in between the Don and Volga rivers. It was to create a strong point in or near Stalingrad to provide protection for the exposed northeastern flank of the troops advancing south into the Caucasus.

Hitler advised von Kleist, who commanded the First Panzer Army, that his troops were to lead the efforts to take the oil centers. Von Kleist cautioned Hitler that if he proceeded that far south, his extended northern and eastern flanks would be extremely vulnerable to Soviet counterstrikes. Hitler reassured him that these areas would be protected by allied troops from Italy, Romania, and Hungary, in addition to the German troops who would control Stalingrad.[59]

The Advance to the Caucasus

Somewhat surprisingly, the Soviets, not the Germans, began aggressive actions in the summer of 1942. Marshal Timoshenko, who now commanded the Ukrainian Front, started the attacks in mid-June, aiming to retake Kharkov. The objectives of the Soviet forces were too ambitious. In early July, the Germans launched counterattacks. They quickly drove back the Soviet armies and encircled about 150,000 of those farthest advanced. Timoshenko's aggressive moves benefited the Germans because the substantial Soviet losses deprived them of troops to resist the planned German offensive. Stalin believed that the German summer offensive would be directed against Moscow. Even following the defeat of Timoshenko's troops in late June, Stalin remained convinced that Moscow would be the target, and that the German moves in the Ukraine were a feint. As a result, the major part of the Soviet armies remained north of Voronezh, ready to defend Moscow.

In early July, the Fourth Panzer Army, commanded by General Hermann Hoth, advanced east to Voronezh on the Don River. Rather than turning north, as the Soviet command expected, Hoth then proceeded south toward Stalingrad. He was followed by the Sixth Army under the command of General Von Paulus, one of the main architects of Barbarossa in 1940. While this operation took place, von Kleist had advanced from Kharkov south to the area between the Donetz and Don rivers. His First Panzer Army crossed the Don east of Rostov and proceeded into the Caucasus. The Seventeenth Army started near Taganrog on the Black Sea, took Rostov and continued south along the eastern shore of the Sea of Azov, with the objective of taking Novorossiysk and Tuapse on the northeastern shore of the Black Sea.

Von Kleist had made rapid progress, but shortly after his advanced troops crossed into the Caucasus, things slowed. Hitler had suddenly decided that the Fourth Panzer Army was not needed for the Stalingrad move and should join von Kleist's forces in the Caucasus. This caused a traffic tie-up on the weak road system, which could not handle another one thousand or so tanks and close to 120,000 supporting infantry, in addition to von Kleist's forces. As a result, the advance of both panzer groups came to an almost complete stop. Two weeks later, Hitler changed his mind and decided that the Fourth Panzer Army should go back to assist the Sixth Army in taking Stalingrad. Hoth's forces got out of the traffic jam and again turned east, and von Kleist's advance south picked up speed. Hitler's interference delayed the move south toward the oilfield and allowed the Soviets time to strengthen the defense of Stalingrad.

A few weeks later, the First Panzer Army again had to stop. The Germans had overcome Russian resistance, but they had run out of fuel. The Russian roads were poor, and as in 1941, the German heavy trucks were not up to the task of providing enough supplies to the fast mobile forces. The Germans tried to use the Russian railroad system, but this required additional work because the tracks of the Russian railroads were wider than those of the German rails. They even used airdrops, but their aircraft could only provide a minor proportion of the needed supply. Following another week's delay, the First Panzer Army was able to resume its advance.

While von Kleist's troops were advancing into central and eastern Caucasus, the Seventeenth Army had made good progress toward Novorossiysk and Tuapse. Its objectives were expanded to include Batumi, a major Soviet naval base, in the Black Sea's southeastern corner. By August 7, the First Panzer Army had reached Maikop, the closest oil center. Von Kleist's forces now covered a very long frontier from Maikop in the west, through Stavropol and Pyatigorsk in the center, toward Grozny, the other oil center north of the Caucasus Mountains in the east.

At this time, Winston Churchill was making his first visit to Joseph Stalin in Moscow, accompanied by three senior commanders, including Army Chief of Staff Alan Brooke and Archibald Wavell, in charge of the Eight Army in Egypt. Churchill's visit was primarily aimed at explaining to Stalin why a British-American invasion of France in 1943 was impossible. However, toward the end of the meeting, Churchill asked Stalin if he thought the Soviet Army could stop the German advance through the Caucasus Mountains toward Baku. Stalin responded that the Soviet Army had twenty-five divisions stationed south of the mountains. He was certain that the Germans would be stopped. Churchill related that he was 50 percent convinced, but that Brooke and Wavell were dubious.[60] Their respect for German military power remained high.

In fact, at that time, the First Panzer Army was close to the end of its capability. It was short of troops, tanks, and fuel. Some of its forces, including, literally, all its air support, had been diverted to the Stalingrad struggle. Nonetheless, during September and October, von Kleist launched one attack after another over a front stretching three hundred kilometers. Grozny was the main target. The Germans managed to take Mozdok about fifty kilometers away, but they could not reach Grozny. The stiffening Soviet resistance and the shortage of fuel caused all German efforts to fail. While the two oil centers north of the mountain chain were important, they only produced about 10 percent of the petroleum from the Caucasus region. The rest came from Baku on the southeastern coast of the Caspian Sea, south of the mountains. Baku, of course, was the ultimate goal of the Caucasus campaign, and in reality, the only rational reason for Hitler's 1942 summer offensive. The German armies, particularly von Kleist's First Panzer Army, had made tremendous progress since the start of the offensive in late June. However, in early November, it was obvious that they would never reach Baku. On November 14, the Soviet counteroffensive began over a wide front.

The Stalingrad Struggle

In early August 1942, von Paulus' Sixth German Army advanced south in the corridor between the Don and Volga rivers. By mid-August, the advanced troops of von Paulus's army had reached the outskirts of Stalingrad at about the same time as Hoth's Fourth Panzer Army started attacking the city from the southwest. Had Hitler not diverted Hoth several weeks earlier, his troops might have entered Stalingrad while the Soviet defenders were unprepared and lacking both manpower and supplies. At that time, Stalingrad might have been taken without much of a fight.

Stalingrad is located on the western shore of the Volga River, so reinforcement and supplies for the few troops who initially defended the city had to cross the river. During this early period, the German aircraft allocated to the Sixth Army, under the command of General Richthofen, were most effective in disrupting Soviet supply efforts. Nonetheless, the Soviet persisted, and by the time the Sixth Army entered Stalingrad in force, there were substantial defending forces in place. In addition, the Soviets enlisted the local population to help in the defense. They responded strongly, both male and female.[61]

As indicated, Stalingrad was not the main objective for the German 1942 summer offensive. Its location between the Don and Volga rivers made it a potential stronghold for the Germans. It would protect the exposed northeast flank of von Kleist's troops. Originally, that was the extent of Stalingrad's role, and there were other locations that could have served as flank protection. However, the name of the city made it an irresistible symbol for Stalin as well as for Hitler. The residents of Stalingrad, plus hundreds of thousands of soldiers from both sides, suffered and died largely because of the limitless egos of two tyrannical dictators.

The battle for the city became very intense and bloody. The German forces launched attacks continuously. They were relatively small actions in separate parts of the city, sometimes supported by a few tanks. They took place in the streets, often hand-to-hand, to gain control of local neighborhoods. The Soviet defenders were eventually pushed back, and by mid-October, they held on to only a narrow strip along the Volga River. However, the Germans could not dislodge the defenders from the strip, and the Soviet troops were gradually being reinforced by troops crossing the river.[62]

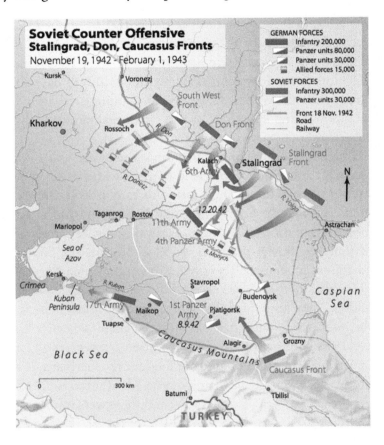

Such was the situation on November 14 when Zhukov launched a counteroffensive. With armored forces in the lead, the Soviet attacks took place both north and south of Stalingrad. The long frontier extended six hundred kilometers from Voronezh south to Stalingrad. It was defended almost entirely by troops allied with the Germans; Italians, Hungarians, and Romanians. The frontier south of Stalingrad was defended primarily by Romanian troops. Many of these allies fought well, but they lacked training and had very little heavy equipment. They could not long withstand the superior Soviet forces. Within a few weeks, the Soviet attacking prongs from the south and the north of the city had joined up some fifty kilometers west of Stalingrad. Any retreat for the Sixth Army was no longer possible. Had von Paulus responded quickly, he might have been able to get some of his troops out of the city in time. But that sort of action was not an option. Hitler would not permit it.

The Germans created a new Army Group Don. It consisted of troops from the Eleventh Army and armored divisions from two panzer armies. In mid-December, Army Group Don, commanded by Field Marshal von Manstein, launched an attempt to relieve the Sixth Army. Von Manstein's troops advanced northeasterly between hostile forces from an area south of the Don. They came within fifty kilometers of a part of the Sixth Army, but at that point, they were stopped by superior Soviet forces. Army Group Don was attacked from both the north and the south and had to retreat to avoid being encircled. The remnants of von Paulus's Sixth Army—about ninety-five thousand of an original force of perhaps three hundred thousand—eventually surrendered in February 1943.

The Perilous Escape of the First Panzer Army

When Zhukov's big counteroffensive started north and south of Stalingrad, other Soviet forces, advancing from the south of the Caucasus mountain range, began attacking von Kleist's First Panzer Army. A Romanian mountain division, part of von Kleist's troops, retreated with heavy losses. As a result, the First Panzer Army terminated its attacks and concentrated on holding its gains. In late November, the two German armies in Army Group A defended a frontier of three hundred kilometers in the northern part of the Caucasus range.

Following the success of Zhukov's offensive both north and south of Stalingrad and the failure of the efforts to relieve the Sixth Army, it was clear that trying to advance farther into the Caucasus mountains was not an option for Army Group A. Merely remaining in the positions these two armies controlled in late November was becoming increasingly hazardous. These troops were located more than five hundred kilometers southeast of Rostov, which offered the sole route for a retreat out of the Caucasus. A retreat would have made sense, but Hitler would not allow it.

In the first week of January 1943, Soviet forces took Mozdok, the easternmost strong point of the First Panzer Army; and a few days later, they took Nalchik, a strong point further west. At the same time, Soviet troops advancing from the area south of Stalingrad crossed the steppe, passed Elista, and approached the eastern end of the Monych Lake, almost three hundred kilometers north of von Kleist's remaining strongholds. These Soviet forces were aiming for Armavir, a key location on the highway connecting Army Group A with Rostov.

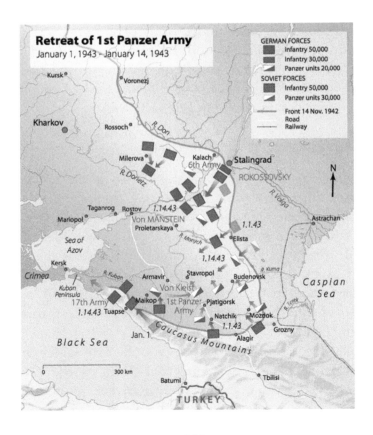

The situation von Kleist was in at this point bore striking similarities to that of Napoleon east of the Berezina River in November of 1812. Strong enemy forces advancing from three sides threatened both. Napoleon had a hard time crossing the Berezina. Von Kleist did not face any such difficulty, but his Army was much farther from relative safety than the French Army. Still, more than a month following the encirclement of the Sixth Army, Hitler prohibited any retreat. Von Kleist was a good deal more obedient to these orders than a general like Guderian might have been. Von Kleist was eventually rewarded, but his compliance came close to spelling total disaster for his armies. Finally, on January 14, Hitler relented and permitted retreat.

Von Kleist had been promoted to command of the entire Army Group A. He ordered the Seventeenth Army to retreat west along the Kuban River toward the Taman Peninsula to keep enough roads open for the retreat north of his armored forces. The Seventeenth Army would eventually cross over to Kerch on the Crimean peninsula. On January 20, von Kleist's Panzer Army was positioned along the Kuma River around 150 kilometers south of Soviet forces pushing west from Elista. About a week later, Von Kleist's troops had passed Armavir, just in time to avoid being cut off by the Soviet Elista force.

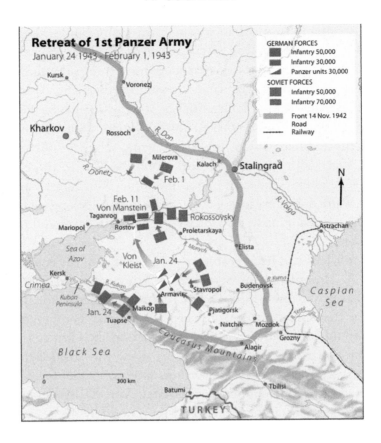

However, the First Panzer Army was still far from safe. General Rokossovsky led a strong Soviet force advancing from Stalingrad south of the Don toward Rostov. They were held off by von Manstein's troops. Following its failed attempt to relieve von Paulus in December, Army Group Don remained in positions as close to Stalingrad as possible to facilitate air support to von Paulus's troops. In January, von Manstein got an even more important responsibility, that of keeping a passage of retreat open for the First Panzer Army. Toward the end of January 1943, Rokossovsky's troops had pushed Army Group Don back to locations only eighty kilometers east of Rostov, but the group defended its positions against continuous attacks by superior Soviet forces. By February 1, von Kleist's troops had passed through the passage east of Rostov and crossed the Don. With his forces finally in reasonable safety, von Kleist had to send a few divisions back to assist von Manstein's hard-pressed troops in their retreat.

Hard fighting continued along the crumbling German front stretching all the way from the Don River's southern bend north to Voronezh. Soviet forces advanced across the land area between the Don and the Donetz rivers, crossed the Donetz, and continued 150 kilometers west of that river, in the process capturing German strongholds such as Kharkov, Belgorod, and Kursk. However, by early March, the Soviet forces were slowed by increasing supply problems as had happened to von Kleist's First Panzer Army in its rapid advance into the Caucasus. Von Manstein's Group Don, which now included most of the First and Fourth Panzer Armies, took advantage of the Soviet stagnation in quick counterattacks, which drove the Soviets back east of the Donetz River and enabled the Germans to retake Belgorod and Kharkov.

Marshal Konstantin Rokossovsky

Konstantin Rokossovsky was born in Warsaw, Poland, to Russian parents in 1896. He was drafted into the tsarist Army in 1914. Following the revolution, he joined the Bolshevik party and served as a cavalry officer in the civil war. During the 1920s and 1930s, he advanced in the Red army, where he became an early advocate of tanks and mobile warfare and reached the rank of lieutenant general in 1937. Possibly his connection to Marshal Tukhachevsky made him suspect in the eyes of Stalin, and Rokossovsky was arrested and charged with treason in August 1937. Despite torture, he refused to sign a confession and was released in 1940.[63] Marshal Timoshenko, then head of the Army and extremely short of qualified officers, put Rokossovsky in charge of a cavalry division. He quickly advanced and played a critical role in senior positions in all the major battles from the start of Barbarossa until the end of World War II. Rokossovsky held positions in both the Soviet and the Polish governments following the war. He died in 1968.

By the middle of March 1943, the front had stabilized. It then ran in almost the same place as when the German summer offensive of 1942 started. Von Kleist's and von Manstein's skillful and persistent efforts had saved the German Army from another defeat, just as catastrophic as the one at Stalingrad. Nevertheless, the German summer offensive, carried out at great cost in personnel as well as equipment, had gained the Germans nothing.

Kursk, the Last Major Offensive

The long struggle for Stalingrad was one of the most dramatic events of the German-Soviet battle and has been the subject of much writing. However, it cannot be considered decisive. For one thing, the German 1942 offensive was not aimed at a final victory in terms of destruction of the Soviet military. The purpose was to gain Germany access to oil. The losses of Germany and its allies were huge, but so were those of the Soviet Union. However, the defeat at Stalingrad and the German retreat from the Caucasus raised a serious question concerning the relative strength of the parties. Until this point in the war, it appeared that the Germans' greater skill in tactical operations, particularly in relation to armored forces, enabled them to launch major attacks at various places on the long frontier. Whether such attacks were intended to be decisive, they created an image of the German troops as a dangerous invading force. Following Stalingrad and the retreat from the Caucasus, did the Germans still retain enough power to successfully implement major attacks?

This question was answered during the battle around Kursk in July 1943. This has been described as the biggest tank battle in history. As a result of the Soviet offensives and the German counteroffensives during February and early March, two salients had developed in the front line. The southern one around Kursk, held by Soviet troops, protruded 150 kilometers west. Bordering it to the north, another salient of about the same size protruded east. This one was defended by German forces and centered on Orel, an important railroad connection with a link directly to Moscow.

Hitler believed a German offensive and a big victory were necessary to restore faith in German power among his own troops and those of his allies. Moreover, he thought a victory could regain for Germany the initiative in the struggle and perhaps even make possible another advance into the Caucasus.[64] The plan was to launch simultaneous attacks against the Kursk salient from the north by Army

Group Central and from the south by the recreated Army Group South, consisting of the former Army Group Don, the Fourth Panzer Army, and some additional mobile forces. A swift breakthrough of Soviet defenses would allow the two German forces to meet at Kursk and hopefully encircle a large number of Soviet defenders. Kursk was located almost in the middle of the salient. To reach Kursk, each of the attacking forces would have to advance about fifty kilometers.

Before either side launched any major attacks, Molotov, the Soviet foreign minister, met with his German counterpart, von Ribbentrop, in Kirovograd in the Ukraine to explore a possible termination of hostilities. The negotiations failed. Von Ribbentrop suggested that the new Soviet western border should run along the Dnieper River, which was not acceptable to Molotov. He insisted that the original Soviet border had to be restored.[65] None of Hitler's senior commanders shared his rosy belief in the prospects of a new offensive. In fact, most would have preferred no new German offensive and instead a retreat to a more defendable front line farther west.[66] Von Manstein, now in command of Army Group South, was an exception and initially favored an offensive. He thought it essential that it start early, preferably in March or April of 1943. He suspected the Soviets would anticipate a German move against the Kursk salient, and delay would enable them better to prepare their defenses.

Deliveries of the new German Panther and Tiger tanks, the answer to the T-34, had finally started. Their development had taken two years, but they were superior fighting vehicles. The Panther, a medium tank, with fifty-millimeter armor protection, a long seventy-five-millimeter gun and good speed and maneuverability, has been considered by many the best tank produced during World War II. The Tiger was a very heavy vehicle with armor so thick that it could withstand almost any frontal hits, and it had an eighty-eight-millimeter gun. However, it was slow. By March 1943, only a few hundred of these tanks had been delivered to the troops in the Ukraine. Despite von Manstein's objections, Hitler decided to delay the offensive until early July to allow more tanks to be delivered.[67]

The force Germany managed to assemble for this event was as big as the one applied in the attack against Moscow in November to December 1941, around nine hundred thousand men, and the armored portion with 3,500 tanks was substantially bigger. In addition, the quality and power of the tanks were much greater. The artillery consisted of ten thousand pieces, mostly anti-tank guns, and Luftwaffe provided support by about two thousand aircraft. The German forces were split almost equally between Army Group Central and Army Group South. This was the most powerful force the Germans had allocated to any one front section.

The delay to July did make a difference. Marshal Zhukov was in overall command of Soviet forces in this area, and Generals Rokossovsky, Vatutin, and Koniev assisted him. Zhukov was sure that the Germans were going to launch an offensive, and that Kursk would be the target. While he was determined to begin attacks against the German salient around Orel, he thought it preferable to let the Germans start. That way, he thought, the Soviet defense could exhaust the attacking German divisions and destroy enough tanks to make the subsequent Soviet offensive easier. Stalin had initially wanted to strike first but was persuaded by Zhukov's arguments. Available Soviet forces in this area were twice the size of the Germans; two million men, around seven thousand tanks and more than twenty thousand pieces of artillery.[68] Supporting Soviet aircraft included 2,500 planes, a little more than Luftwaffe's force. Zhukov prepared very extensive minefields and other tank obstacles, and put in place numerous anti-tank guns, all in the areas where he calculated the German attacks would take place.

On July 5, 1943, the German offensive against the Kursk salient started from north and south. Von Kluge's Army Group Central attacked with several infantry division in a narrow front. The intent was to create a break in the defense, which the tanks could then exploit. The northern section of the salient was defended by Rokossovsky's troops. They were well prepared, assisted in part by British intelligence concerning the date and time of the attack. The Soviet minefields and artillery proved formidable obstacles for the attacking troops. Unlike in 1941, the Soviet Air Force was effective in preventing Luftwaffe from giving the German forces much support. After six days of intensive fighting, sometimes hand-to-hand as at Stalingrad, von Kluge was stopped without having penetrated more than the first Soviet defensive lines and with an advance of only about six kilometers.

Von Manstein's Army Group South, attacking the Kursk salient from the south, ran into the same difficulties as Army Group Central. Army Group South was a bit more successful than von Kluge's forces, but by July 12, the southern attack had been stopped as well, with a penetration into the salient of about twenty kilometers. The German attackers were stopped before they were even close to accomplishing their objective of connecting at Kursk and encircling Soviet troops. In fact, Zhukov had taken precautions to avoid this danger by moving a large proportion of the Soviet troops out of the salient before the German attacks.

On July 12, Rokossovsky and Vatutin launched the Soviet counteroffensives. Rokossovsky attacked north from the Kursk salient into the Orel salient, supported by other Soviet forces attacking from north of this salient. Army Group Center put up a vigorous defense, and the new Tiger and Panther tanks proved very effective in tank battles. Nonetheless, by early August, Rokossovsky's troops had conquered the entire salient, including the city of Orel.

Vatutin, attacking south from the Kursk salient and supported by Konev's troops, advancing across the Donetz River farther south, quickly encircled Kharkov and pushed the front line two hundred kilometers west. By August 15, it was running just a little east of Poltava.

For Hitler, the Kursk offensive was extremely important, but he must have realized that it was quite a gamble. A German victory would restore confidence among his troops and create the potential for further offensives. By August 15, 1943, these hopes and expectations were gone. Hitler had made his commanders put together the biggest and most powerful force in terms of manpower, armor, artillery, and aircraft that the German military was still capable of. However, the offensive was a complete failure. The German troops had fought well, and the armored forces, including the new tanks, had been as effective as could have been expected. The enemy was simply too strong.

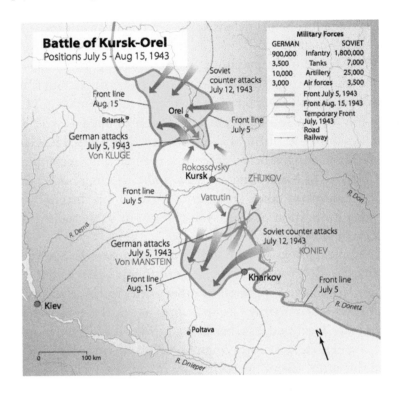

It was not just that the Soviets had great superiority in infantry as well as armored forces. It was also the fact that the Soviet commanders on almost every level had learned and were now able to perform with almost the same competence as the Germans. The gap in skill, which had been so crucial to the German victories in 1941 and 1942, was not totally gone, but it was nowhere nearly as significant as during Barbarossa and even the early parts of the 1942 Caucasus campaign. The conclusion from the results of the Kursk-Orel struggle in July 1943 was clear. The German invading armies had now been reduced to the level in which Napoleon's Grand Army found itself when departing from Moscow in October 1812. They were no longer a fearful invading force, capable of conquering and endangering enemy land and industry. They were now foreign troops trying to hold their positions as long as they could in a hostile country, against the attacks of an increasingly superior opponent.

The war between Germany and the Soviet Union went on for almost another two years. However, following the battles at Kursk-Orel, the Germans did not attempt a significant offensive. Accordingly, the end of that battle appears a suitable conclusion to this account of the campaign that Hitler launched in June 1941.

Why Barbarossa and the 1942 Offensive Failed

Inaccurate Evaluations

The failure of Barbarossa and the subsequent failures of German offensives against the Soviet Union produced as much surprise as had the inability of Napoleon and Charles XII to defeat their Russian enemies. In June of 1941, Germany seemed to possess the perfect war machine. It was scoring quick and easy victories wherever it was engaged in Europe. In comparison, the Soviet military was generally thought to be in dismal condition. As indicated above, Stalin's purges of most of his best senior officers, and the weak performance of the Soviet Army in the Winter War with Finland (1939–40) appeared to justify that evaluation. Hitler and Germans in general, encouraged by the intense efforts by Goebbels and his cohorts, were convinced that Barbarossa would be a short and easy campaign. In developing the plans for Barbarossa, Hitler as well as Halder, von Paulus, and other officers involved thought it purely up to the German high command to decide when and how the Soviet armies would be defeated. Plans and actions by the Soviet forces were considered as more or less irrelevant.[69]

So why did the Germans fail? The gross underestimation of Soviet forces and their fighting ability and the tremendous obstacles provided by Russian nature and weather would be a quick answer, but a more detailed analysis is called for. Before launching Barbarossa in June of 1941, Hitler and his commanders had tried to evaluate relevant aspects of the Soviet military; its size, quality, leadership, and likely strategy. Their conclusions were not wrong in all areas. They correctly assumed that Stalin's purges had resulted in a severe shortage of competent commanders and that individuals of modest ability and/or insufficient training would occupy important positions in the defending Army. This was in particular true in respect to the commanders and crews of the armored forces and the leaders of the Air Force.

Many other critical conclusions were drastically wrong. The Soviet Union had a much bigger Air Force and many more and better tanks than the Germans assumed. Some tanks were superior to even the best the Germans employed. The willingness and capability of the rank and file of the Soviet army to fight were far greater than the Germans had expected. The Soviet industry would not be so easy to conquer or destroy because Stalin had begun moving it toward the Ural area long before the German attack.

The Germans realized that the size of the Soviet Union could become a problem, which is why Hitler insisted that victory should be won west of the Dnieper River. The German leadership, however, had little knowledge of the nature of the Russian roads, and the impact the weather might have on those roads. Their inaccurate conclusions concerning the location of the Soviet industry made them think decisive battles could be expected reasonably close to the border. Stalin and Zhukov would, of course, try to protect important areas, wherever located in the country, but they would not allow the Soviet Army to be destroyed in a few big battles in the western part of the country.

Hitler's assumption that the Soviet forces could be decisively defeated west of the Dnieper-Dvina line turned out to be as inaccurate as Napoleon's expectations of a quick victory. Von Bock's Army Group Central did take Minsk in less than two weeks, but a big proportion of the defending forces escaped. Despite its many serious weaknesses, the Soviet military was able to launch counterattacks to an extent the Germans had never expected. Halder and the other German planners had also greatly underestimated the availability of Soviet reserves.[70]

Insufficient and Inadequate Equipment

Because Stalin and his commanders were able to withdraw the bulk of the Soviet Army far into their country, great pressure was put on the German transportation system. Fuel and other supplies had to keep pace with the fast moving panzer forces in order for the offensives to be sustainable. The same was true of the infantry divisions, by far, the biggest part of the invading armies. They had to support the panzer groups in breaking Soviet defensive positions and resisting counterattacks. Meeting these challenges turned out to be difficult right from the start.

The Russian railroads had wider tracks than those of the Germans, so unless enough Russian railroad equipment could be captured at an early stage, the rails had to be redone. In the meantime, the Germans depended on heavy trucks to provide both supplies to their armored forces and to move up the infantry. The German invading Army had too few trucks, and they were not adequately equipped for the poor Russian roads.

The mobile forces of Army Group Central did advance rapidly and in early July 1941 started the big encirclement in the Smolensk area. However, many of the Soviet troops were able to escape, before Guderian and Hoth could close the pocket. Marshal Timoshenko kept launching continuous attacks against Guderian and Hoth's advanced forces. The greatly outnumbered armored forces, without infantry support and short of ammunition, were in an almost desperate situation. What had been expected to be a fast and easy battle, lasted for almost a month before von Bock declared the pocket closed. Even then it was not quite true because Soviet troops kept slipping out. The victory was still a remarkable achievement, primarily by the two German panzer groups.

However, the difficulty and cost of this success came as a big shock to the Germans. The unquestioned optimism, which had characterized the attitude of Hitler and his commanders at the start of Barbarossa, was gone. Halder, von Brauchitsch, and von Bock were all worried. Hitler seemed confused and uncertain. Goebbels concluded that a more cautious reporting to the German people was called for. The victory at Smolensk was significant but far from decisive. It was now clear that to complete Barbarossa successfully the German forces would have to resolve problems, which so far they had not been able to handle, including that of transportation.

The Army Was Not Strong Enough

During the final planning stage of Barbarossa, Hitler had declared that the German forces were adequate to accomplish the plan to totally destroy the Soviet Army and industry. None of his commanders objected, although von Paulus, a key member of the planning team, had serious doubts. Hitler retained full confidence in Barbarossa even though von Kleist's armor, part of Army Groups South, was not at full strength as a result of the Balkan diversion. Overall, the German armored forces in June 1941 were nowhere near as strong as was generally assumed at the time. Army Group Central, had a total of 1,900 tanks. Of these, one-half were Panzer 1 and Panzer 2, outmoded models that were too weak to contribute much if serious resistance was encountered.

Thanks to his weak but skillfully managed armored forces, von Bock had won the victory at Smolensk, but the losses suffered by these troops were close to disastrous. Guderian's group had 970 tanks at the start of Barbarossa. According to Stahel, after Smolensk in early August 1941, only 370 remained operational. Another 350 or so could be restored to serviceability, but they needed significant repair and maintenance. The situation at Hoth's group was about the same.[71] Clearly, a renewal of the offensive toward Moscow was impossible until these needs had been satisfied. Some critical spare parts, engines for the tanks for instance, were hard to come by.

There were signs already in August 1941 that the success of Barbarossa had become questionable. Some key German commanders were worried. General Kesselring, head of the Luftwaffe fleet assigned to Army Group Center, noted in his diary that the Panzer groups in particular were too small to accomplish Barbarossa's objectives. Kesselring maintained that even Luftwaffe was pushed beyond its capabilities.[72]

In early August, von Brauchitsch managed to convince Hitler that a period of rest for the troops and service of the vehicles and equipment was necessary. On August 3, Hitler flew to Borisov (a critical town during Napoleon's 1812 retreat) to meet with the top commanders of Army Group Central. In addition to other discussions, Guderian and Hoth had an opportunity to plead with Hitler for speedy delivery of spare parts and some of the recently produced new tanks. Hitler allowed them four hundred engines and thirty-five tanks. Following this meeting, Guderian had to use his thinning forces for a quick move to the Kiev area to help von Rundstedt complete the big encirclement of Budyonny's troops. Then the Second Panzer group returned north and joined the offensive against Moscow. It is hardly surprising that by late November, Guderian's remaining tanks were too few to accomplish his objectives at Tula.

Some of the German generals said later that Barbarossa could have succeeded had Hitler not delegated Guderian's Panzer Group 2 in early August to support von Rundstedt's Army Group South. But their opinions are not entirely convincing. While that decision did delay the final offensive, Guderian's and Hoth's panzer groups simply did not have enough operational tanks left for an offensive all the way to Moscow. Had the offensive started in late August instead of late September, and had the armored forces somehow managed to enter Moscow, most likely they would have been driven out by Zhukov's counteroffensive.

Despite the heavy losses in manpower and equipment suffered by the Soviet Army, it was far from defeated in October to November 1941. In order to win his hesitant commanders' support for the final offensive against Moscow, Hitler had claimed that the Soviet army was near collapse. The strength and size of Zhukov's counteroffensive in December caused a near panic among the German troops. Their commanders were caught by surprise because they had continued to underestimate the Soviet forces.

Barbarossa did not fail because of some major German strategic or tactical error. It failed because the attacking armies, especially the armored groups, were not large enough, and the German forces could not meet the need for timely supply and support required by the front line. As a result, the fast-moving panzer forces, demonstrating great skill in dealing with numerically superior enemy troops, did not get the fuel, ammunition, and other supplies they needed, and too often had to do without supporting infantry.

The Offensive in 1942 Was Wrong

Despite Germany's failure to win a decisive victory in 1941, most observers expected that a German spring or summer offensive in 1942 would finish off the Soviet forces. As indicated above, a big new offensive was not an approach favored by most of the senior German commanders, and Hitler was hesitant.

Stalin and the Soviet high command expected a German offensive in the early part of 1942. They thought it would be aimed at Moscow. There was little reason for Stalin and Zhukov to strike first. Time was working in their favor. The longer the inaction lasted, the more time they got to strengthen and train the fairly fresh troops, who had replaced the losses during 1941. The armored forces, in particular, could be greatly improved. Although Hitler refused to believe it, German intelligence had established that the Soviets produced many more tanks than the German industry. Clearly, inaction on the eastern front was not in the interest of Germany, and Hitler was vehemently opposed to any form of retreat. So Hitler's decision, once he made up his mind, to commence a new offensive was hardly surprising and was logical under the circumstances.

However, the new offensive's objective to conquer the oil fields in the Caucasus was wrong. The Caucasus plan was much too ambitious considering the logistic aspects and available German resources. It was totally unrealistic to expect that it would produce a favorable result. An even greater problem was that this plan eliminated the opportunity to win the war. This required a decisive defeat of the Soviet military followed by destruction or control of its industry. The major part of the Soviet Army was positioned to defend against a possible attack against Moscow. Accordingly, to win the war, the Germans had to renew the offensive against Moscow and encircle and destroy the Soviet troops defending the city. By instead directing the attack toward the remote oil fields, a lengthy war was guaranteed, even if the new German offensive was completely successful. In view of the Soviet superiority in manpower, its industry's ability to meet crucial needs of its military and increasing aid from the United States and the United Kingdom, a lengthy war was not likely to be won by the Germans.

Why did Hitler decide on the Caucasus option rather than another attack against Moscow? Did he have doubts about the ability of his forces to defeat the main Soviet armies? Or did he think that the Caucasus offensive would be a way of winning the war? Hitler was known to have retained his exaggerated expectation of the German forces, which had been typical of him and many of his senior commanders in 1940–41. And like Charles XII, he never seems to have developed any respect for the power and ability of his enemies. Maybe, even now, in the spring of 1942, he still thought the German armies could accomplish whatever he directed them to do. Perhaps he thought his forces could not only secure oil for Germany, but also deny it for the Soviets.[73] That way, the war might be won. If those had been his thoughts, they were, of course, nothing but dreams.

Why did his senior advisors not put Hitler on the right track? Primarily because most of them were gone. He had fired von Brauchischts, the commander in chief of the Army, and also von Rundstedt and von Leeb in command of Army Groups South and North, respectively. Von Bock, in command of Army Group Central, was on sick leave. Guderian had been fired for insubordination, and von Paulus, formerly Halder's deputy, was now leading the Sixth Army. Only Halder remained of what might have been thought of as the brain trust behind Barbarossa. Hitler and Halder had never had a very good relationship. While Halder participated actively in the planning and guidance of the Caucasus campaign until he was fired in August 1942, it is unlikely that Hitler would have been swayed by any ideas Halder might have had that differed from his own.[74]

Hitler and His Commanders

Hitler as a Commander

Hitler's principal exposure to war before 1939 was his lengthy experience in the trenches in World War I. Although he was promoted to corporal, it is doubtful that he learned anything of value. Possibly his later interest in mobile forces was a desire to avoid the stationary warfare he had experienced before.

Some observers have felt that Hitler had an amazing feel and talent for politics. It was demonstrated on his way to power and subsequently by his successful promotion of his aggressive ideas domestically as well as in international areas.[75] It should be recognized that the almost complete paralysis of Great Britain and France was a major reason for the European slide into chaotic conditions. However, Hitler's skillful maneuvering during the seven years prior to 1939 must get a good deal of credit for the gradual success of his evil designs.

The victory in France in 1940 persuaded him that he possessed superior talents for military tactics and strategy. Hitler had encouraged and supported the use of the panzer forces advocated by Guderian and his allies despite reservations expressed by many senior German commanders. The exaggerated praise from Field Marshal Keitel, at the top of the German military hierarchy, contributed to Hitler's increasingly unrealistic estimate of his own capability. Halder, von Brauchitsch, and particularly von Rundstedt undoubtedly felt quite differently about Hitler's ability, but they limited themselves to occasionally questioning his military proposals. Von Rundstedt was the strongest voice cautioning against Barbarossa, but he was not alone. Clearly, things might have worked out very differently if Hitler had paid more attention to the Barbarossa skeptics.

Hitler's decisions regarding events important for Germany are critical in evaluating him as a military commander. As a dictator, Hitler had the ultimate responsibility for all major actions taken by Germany. He failed badly in regard to the two most important decisions in the conflict with the Soviet Union: the one to start the invasion in 1941 and the one to launch the 1942 offensive in the Caucasus instead of against Moscow.

Hitler also made a political decision that was unfortunate for Germany. Following Pearl Harbor, the Unites States declared war on Japan, but not on Germany. On December 8, 1941, the Japanese Ambassador to Germany suggested to von Ribbentrop, the German Foreign Minister, that Germany join the war against the United States and its allies. Under the Axis Pact between Germany, Italy, and Japan, a party was obligated to aid another party attacked by a third party. This obligation did not apply if the other Axis party was the aggressor. Von Ribbentrop was not happy about the ambassador's suggestion, fearing it might hurt Germany's war in Russia. Hitler, however, enthusiastically went along with the proposal. To the parliament, he described the idea of Germany declaring war on the United States as a great opportunity for Germany. The reality was exactly the opposite.

The war in the Atlantic was intense, and the German submarines were extremely successful in inflicting losses on allied convoys to Britain as well as to the Soviet Union. In order to protect its submarine fleet, Germany needed to keep the United States out of the battle as long as possible. Of course, following Pearl Harbor, Roosevelt could be expected to intensify his efforts to get the United States into the war against Germany, but there were strong isolationist groups in Congress.[76] After the stunning Japanese attack, many Congress members felt that the United States ought to deal first with the Japanese problem before getting involved in a war in Europe. Had Hitler been able to clearly understand Germany's strategic interests, the last thing he would have wanted to do was to declare war against the United States.

The last big German offensive, the one at Kursk in July 1943, must also be considered a strategic error. The offensive involved a huge proportion of Germany's remaining military forces available for the war in the East. The surprise element, considered a critical part of any armored attack according to principles accepted in the German Army, was totally absent.[77] In addition, there was really no clear objective, except trying to show that the German military was still able to carry out a major offensive. The attack was severely criticized by Guderian, who considered it an unaffordable waste of armored forces. Looking at all his major strategic decisions, Hitler's record was weak.

Considering tactical decisions on the battlefield, the supreme commander, located in a headquarters hundreds of kilometers behind the front, ought to rely on his field commanders. Only if matters are clearly going the wrong way is action from the headquarters justified. This, however, was not Hitler's approach. He insisted on micromanaging activities, which caused repeated tactical errors. Stalingrad might have been taken without much of a battle if Hitler had not interfered with the advance of the Fourth Panzer Army in June of 1942. Stalingrad might also have become much less of a total disaster if Hitler had not prohibited any German retreat. The First Panzer Army was almost needlessly sacrificed in the Caucasus due to Hitler's orders to von Kleist to remain where he was. When this order was issued, several months had passed since the Soviet forces had defeated and driven away the troops, mostly Romanian and Italian, allocated to protect von Kleist's retreat from the Caucasus.

In their discussions with Liddell Hart after the war, a number of the German generals indicated that the above examples from the German 1942 and 1943 operations were not exceptions.[78] During the long period from the middle of 1943 until Germany's final defeat in May 1945, the German commanders fought almost continuous defensive battles on the Russian front. The attacking Soviet forces were invariably substantially superior in all relevant aspects, but most of the German commanders had developed effective defensive tactics. Several of them told Liddell Hart they thought they could have held out almost indefinitely and perhaps have exhausted the Soviet armies if it had not been for Hitler's continuous interference. In particular, he insisted on the prohibition of any retreat, even threatening commanders in violation of his orders with court martial.

In conclusion, Hitler was not a good military commander. Germany would have been far better off if somebody like von Rundstedt or von Manstein had been supreme commander.

Hitler's Deadly Ideologies

The gradual implementation of Hitler's racial programs in Germany during the 1930s was fairly well known even outside Germany. Hitler did not seem to try very hard to hide what he was doing. While his policies were criticized abroad, no country suggested any drastic action to protect the victims. No country boycotted the 1936 Olympic Games, which Hitler hosted. In contrast, the United States stayed away from the 1980 Moscow Olympics because of the Soviet invasion of Afghanistan.

As Hitler's criminal programs intensified, persecution in Germany turned into human extermination of Jews, communists, homosexuals, gypsies, and other "undesirables." Germany's enemies plus the neutral countries reacted but were unable to take action to prevent the atrocities until the end of the war. When Barbarossa was about to be launched, Hitler announced to his senior commanders that in this battle, the Geneva Conventions and other restraints on military or occupying forces would not apply. He directed, for instance, that any Soviet commissar taken prisoner should be immediately shot. When the battle in Stalingrad heated up, Hitler issued instructions that all male civilians should be killed. He considered this necessary in order to erase Bolshevism. Hitler's policies in respect to occupied Soviet territory went far beyond individual killings. Special police forces followed the troops in Russia and the Ukraine, rounding up and killing essentially the same groups who were the victims in Germany.

These activities were judged crimes against humanity in the Nuremberg trials in 1948. Most of the major culprits who were still alive were condemned to death and executed, including field marshals Keitel and Jodl. Hitler's policies were not only morally outrageous; they were also counterproductive in relation to the German military campaigns. In the early stages of Barbarossa, planners had assumed that a significant proportion of the civilian population in invaded areas would support the German invaders. This was not implausible. Stalin's policies had in many areas been just as violent and oppressive as those of Hitler, and Stalin maintained harsh policies against the Soviet population even after Barbarossa had begun.[79]

In the Ukraine, a force was created to provide military support for the Germans. However, once the local population came to realize the true nature of the German occupation policy, the enthusiasm for supporting the invaders vanished. Instead, increasingly strong guerilla groups developed, causing the German troops significant difficulties. In the climactic battle around Kursk in July to August 1943, guerilla forces carried out continuous attacks against German railroad and other transportation connections, which significantly inhibited German troop movements. A more humane occupation policy might have made things a good deal easier for the German troops.

The Nature of Wars

Wars are by nature violent. However, the way the military campaigns were conducted in 1707–09, 1812, and 1941–45 differed significantly in how commanders, soldiers, and the civilian populations were treated. It seems clear that the most recent campaign was by far the most violent and ruthless. Hitler's conduct and orders to his commanders were adjudged not only to violate established rules of war, but to constitute gross human rights violations and war crimes. Even Stalin employed measures to control his troops and the civilian population that violated accepted standards and might have received widespread international condemnation if the Soviet Union had not been one of the victors in World War II. Following the fast German conquest of Minsk, the commanding general of that front and his deputy were called to Moscow where they were quickly convicted to death for incompetence.[80] During the Stalingrad battle, numerous commanders, soldiers, and civilians were executed for desertion, incompetence, or failure to fight.

Far less of this kind of violence and fewer human rights violations apparently occurred during Napoleon's and Charles's campaigns. There are few reports of French or Swedish troops engaging in wanton killings of civilians. At one time, Napoleon wrote to Kutuzov asking him to assist in conducting the war in a more humane manner.[81] When Lewenhaupt finally arrived at the Swedish headquarters at Propolsk after Lesnaya with all supplies and half of his troops lost, Charles calmly listened to his account with little criticism and no threats. It is easy to imagine what Lewenhaupt's fate would have been in the Soviet Army in 1941. Peter's treatment of the Swedish prisoners following Poltava was exceptionally tolerant. He gave great recognition to the performance of the senior Swedish commanders, an approach he subsequently repeated on similar occasions and made generous offers to many of the Swedish officers.[82]

Hitler's Commanders

The German commanders on almost all levels of command were well educated and trained. Many of the senior officers belonged to families with long military traditions. Most carried out their duties in an efficient, professional manner. Some, such as von Rundstedt, von Manstein, von Kleist, and Guderian, were exceptionally competent. Nonetheless, there was also a person in a top position like Keitel, who was almost a political hack. Because of his unquestioning support of Hitler, he was despised by most of his fellow commanders.

It is hardly surprising that given their Prussian traditions, many of these generals found it hard to respect Hitler, an upstart without any significant education, who had reached his position of power primarily through his talent as a demagogic orator. Their skepticism about Hitler's judgments and ability as a commander was the reason for Halder's and von Brauchitscht's conspiracies in the fall of 1938. It is equally easy to understand Hitler's dislike of almost all his top commanders, considering his modest background, his homeless experiences in Vienna, and his four years on the front as an ordinary soldier in World War I. The lack of respect on either side must have played a big role in Hitler's continuous destructive interference in matters on the front throughout the war in the East.

The culpability of the military commanders in the atrocities committed by Germany in Russia and the Ukraine deserves some attention. Hitler and the members of his cabinet set the overall policy that authorized and directed war crimes on a wide scale. This included Field Marshal Keitel, as head of the German General Staff and in effect Hitler's minister of war, and also Field Marshal Jodl, Keitel's deputy. While these criminal policies were primarily carried out by special police forces, German commanders on almost all levels must be charged with some responsibility because most of them knew what was going on and did nothing to stop it.

Beginning in 1945, various legal and military authorities closely examined this matter. Eventually, the International Military Tribunal, which performed the Nuremberg trials, decided that besides political leaders, only the German military command as some kind of collective and its two top officers, Keitel and Jodl, would be indicted. As a result, no German field commander was tried at Nuremberg. Keitel and Jodl were both convicted and executed. The tribunal also issued a statement of moral condemnation of many officers, who were assumed to have participated in crimes, although not indicted. Some of the German officers were true Nazis while others had little sympathy for either Hitler or his ideas. However, the moral judgment expressed by the tribunal was well deserved.

Napoleon, Charles and Hitler Compared

The Purpose of the Campaigns

Napoleon's aim was to make Alexander cooperate in the battle with Britain. In addition, Napoleon felt Russia had gradually started departing from important aspects of its relationship with France, established by the Tilsit peace agreement in 1807. By demonstrating the French military superiority, Napoleon believed Alexander would again recognize Russia's status as a junior partner with France and resume compliance with the Continental Accord. In his many peace approaches to Alexander, Napoleon stressed his desire for good relations with Russia as soon as they had settled their differences.

Charles's objective was to recover a small but important section of the Swedish Empire and to humiliate Peter for his attack on Sweden in 1700. Peter's removal was not necessary if Peter cooperated.

Hitler, on the other hand, was aiming for the destruction of the Soviet military and the Soviet government and its ideology, Bolshevism. In addition, he wanted to kill, imprison, or remove many sections and parts of the Soviet population, Jews, gypsies, homosexuals, etc.

With such different goals, it might seem surprising that their military campaigns in many ways were quite similar. All three commanders were hoping for a decisive battle with the main enemy force as quickly and as close to the Russian border as possible. All three knew that advancing too far into Russia might create problems with which they might not be able to cope. However, their strengths as compared to their opponents were not the same, and their operating options were somewhat different.

The Significance of Third Parties

Napoleon, Charles, and Hitler all had to keep in mind third parties and their actual or potential actions. Napoleon had succeeded in turning into allies two of his major enemies, Austria and Prussia. They were even providing assistance to his campaign against Alexander. But the alliances were fragile and the participants' support depended very much on the success of Napoleon's Russian campaign. In addition, French armies were still tied up in the costly military campaign in Spain, facing allied British, Spanish, and Portuguese forces. That war started in 1807 and posed a serious and growing threat.[83]

Charles had made peace with his previous enemies, Denmark and Saxony, and turned Poland into an ally before launching his invasion in 1707. Nonetheless, these agreements were no stronger than those Napoleon had shaped. They were unlikely to hold if the Swedish forces were severely weakened in Russia. In that case, almost all the countries in Northern Europe, even Prussia, would pose a threat to Sweden.

Hitler's situation in respect to third parties was worse than those of Napoleon and Charles. The United Kingdom and its empire were active enemies at the start of Barbarossa, and there was increasing danger that the United Sates might join the war. Britain provided aid to the Soviet Union from the start of the German invasion, and such aid would increase dramatically if the United States became a participant in the hostilities. A victory against the Soviet forces would not eliminate the need to deal with Britain and America, but it would put Germany in a far stronger position. By early 1942, Hitler had made Germany's situation worse by declaring war against the United States. As a result, American military assistance to the Soviet Union increased greatly.

The Leadership

The differences in leadership ability between Napoleon and Charles on the one hand and Hitler on the other were great. Hitler's weakness and lack of a professional approach in running a military campaign have been duly noted. In contrast, Napoleon and Charles were professional soldiers as well as authoritarian rulers when they invaded Russia. In addition, they had long experience. Unlike Hitler, they were continuously close to the action in the field.[84] For the most part, they were able to ensure that their armies made the right moves. The various maneuvers that Charles executed to overcome Peter's resistance during his long advance from Saxony to the Dnieper River and Napoleon's decisive actions and moral support to the struggling engineers during the extreme crises at the Berezina River in November 1812 are good examples. But both Napoleon and Charles committed a few serious strategic errors. And Napoleon was not performing with his usual high skill and energy for much of the Russian campaign.

Most of Hitler's senior field commanders—men like von Rundstedt, von Manstein, Guderian, Halder, and von Kleist—were professional and competent. The same can be said of Napoleon's marshals and the Swedish major generals and colonels who commanded regiments and cavalry squadrons in the Swedish Army. At the very top of the Swedish structure there was, unfortunately, the hostility between Rehnskjöld and Lewenhaupt, which proved so disastrous at Poltava.

Could Any of the Campaigns Have Succeeded?

From the foregoing account, it would seem that Charles's campaign could certainly have succeeded if he had avoided a few crucial strategic errors. Of the three campaigns, his had the best chance for success. He had made his campaign more difficult by aiming it toward Moscow instead of St. Petersburg. But even though Moscow was a substantially more difficult target, the campaign could have succeeded. Unlike in the campaigns of Napoleon and Hitler, Moscow was a crucial target in the struggle between Charles and Peter. Even following Lesnaya, Charles could have saved his Army and the Swedish empire and possibly have won the war if he had moved his Army back to Riga in the late fall of 1708.

Napoleon also could have won and forced Alexander to comply with his wishes, at least for a time. However, in order to realize all of his objectives he depended on the cooperation of Alexander and Barclay de Tolly. Napoleon needed a battle near the Russian border and within a short time of his campaign's start or the Grand Army would incur great losses in securing victory. If the casualties were great, Napoleon would not strengthen his position in Europe. Because he was unable to keep his forces adequately supplied, Napoleon had fewer margins for error than Charles. Until early August in Smolensk, Napoleon could have reached partial success in terms of a costly victory, which might have made Alexander negotiate. However, such a victory would have done nothing to improve Napoleon's overall position in Europe. Napoleon could have avoided the total destruction of the Grand Army if he had decided to terminate the campaign in Smolensk.

Hitler had no second options. He had to defeat the Soviet Army decisively or lose the war. There was no crucial Soviet target within reach of the German forces that could substitute for decisive victory in the field. The conquest of Moscow would not have been enough. Barbarossa's chances of success were poor because Germany did not have the necessary resources to realize the purpose of the campaign.[85] In early 1942, Hitler could have followed von Rundstedt's advice and withdrew the German armies back to the German border. But

Germany still would not have been out of the failed enterprise unless Stalin had been willing to cooperate.

Did Any Campaign Make Sense?

The account so far has described the events as they happened. It also is worth assessing to what extent these difficult, expensive, and very bloody campaigns were sensible from a military or strategic standpoint. In evaluating this issue, it is important to consider both the upside and downside potentials of the campaigns. What benefit did the aggressor expect if the campaign succeeded, and what loss might be incurred if it failed?

Napoleon's decision to invade Russia did not make much sense. He had two principal objectives: make Alexander comply with the Continental System and demonstrate to Alexander and other European rulers that France's military power was such that it should not be challenged. To satisfy both these criteria, Napoleon had to win a decisive victory early in his campaign close to the Russian border, but Alexander and Barclay de Tolly were too competent to allow that to happen.[86] Accordingly, his prospects were poor from the start. In addition, had Napoleon succeeded in getting a new commitment from Alexander to stop trading with Britain, how would Napoleon have been able to enforce it? Compliance would be costly to the Russian economy, and Alexander would undoubtedly have realized that Napoleon hardly had the resources to enforce a new treaty.

So Napoleon's 1812 campaign did not have much of an upside. Napoleon probably had hardly thought of a downside. His army was far superior to anything the Russians could put together, so how could he fail? Nonetheless, by allowing his army to be pulled too far into Russia, a downside developed that was so enormous that Napoleon spent the last years of his life as a prisoner at St. Helena.

In 1812, France had reached and even exceeded its capacity for controlling the many countries of Europe. What Napoleon should have done was to seek a negotiated peace with Britain instead of invading Russia.

Hitler's worst mistake in the war with the Soviet Union was to start the war in the first place. Then, is it possible to argue that the campaign made sense? After the fact, we know that Barbarossa was a bad decision. However, at the time when Hitler, Halder, von Paulus, and few others put together the plans for Barbarossa, things looked quite different to them and many others. And there was a substantial upside to Barbarossa. Had the German military been able to decisively defeat the Soviet army in 1941, it would have put Germany in a very strong position in World War II.

Hitler and a few of his commanders—but far from all—had so excessive a belief in German superiority that they probably had given no thought to a downside of Barbarossa. However, in reality it was huge. Failure to defeat the Soviet military decisively in 1941 or at the latest in the summer of 1942 would cause Germany to lose the war. Because Hitler and his commanders had not done their homework, they engaged the German armies in a campaign that was beyond their capability. So regardless of any potential, Barbarossa made no sense.

The principle purpose of Charles's campaign was quite realistic. The Swedish Army probably could have recovered all the Swedish territory Peter had taken while Charles was busy in Poland and Saxony, regardless of any Russian resistance. Since the territory involved had great strategic significance, the campaign would have made sense. However, this conclusion is based on the assumption that Charles would have chosen the best approach for his campaign. He did not. The optimal approach would have been a move from Altranstädt in Saxony to Swedish territory in Riga and then on toward St. Petersburg. Such a campaign might have had a 70 to 75 percent chance of success.

When Charles instead aimed his campaign against Moscow, the likelihood of success dropped to perhaps 30 percent at the start. Even though the campaign might have succeeded, it did not make sense. In launching a lengthy, costly, and difficult campaign, a commander clearly needs to elect the best possible approach. If Moscow had been the only alternative, or if it had been reasonable for Charles to believe that Moscow was the best choice, his decision might have been judged sensible. But under the circumstances in 1707, Moscow was clearly not the optimal target for the Swedish campaign and Charles undoubtedly knew it. Instead of aiming his campaign against the optimal target, Charles deliberately chose a harder approach. Given his responsibilities as commander in chief and king of Sweden, that made no sense.

So neither Napoleon's, Hitler's, nor Charles's campaigns succeeded, and it is concluded that none of them made sense but for quite different reasons.

FINAL OBSERVATIONS

Napoleon caused a lot of pain and suffering for France, but his memory is still the subject of much interest and appreciation there as well as in the world at large. Both Marshals Ney and Murat were executed by members the Bourbon family when the family returned to power, but the names of both marshals can be found today on the Arc de Triomphe in Paris.

In the same way, Charles XII's immature decisions and stubborn attitude resulted in Sweden suffering great human and economic pain, the loss of key strategic areas and its status as a big power in Northern Europe. Nonetheless, there is a big statue of Charles XII pointing east in a prime location in Stockholm; and in the main church in Mora, a big tourist center in Dalarna, one will find the portraits of two Swedish kings; Gustavus Adolphus and Charles XII.

Perhaps it is not necessary to win all the wars or make the right key decisions to retain fame and appreciation. There appears to be a good deal of nostalgia looking back at the times when the country—whichever country it may be—was famous and powerful. For the common Swedes and for Sweden as a whole, Charles's father, Charles XI, accomplished far more than Charles, but Charles XII was the hero king. However much better his father may have been for Sweden, it is Charles's picture you will find in various public places in Sweden.

There are no statues or commemorations of Hitler or any of his generals in Germany today. The reasons are obvious, and it is to be hoped that things will remain the same for a very long time.

NOTES

1. Napoleon wanted his position as First Consul approved by the General Assembly, but the members were not informed in advance and took offense to Napoleon's presence among them.

2. Chandler, *The Campaigns of Napoleon*, 260–61. Jean-Baptiste Bernadotte, a General of Division and former Minister of War in November of 1799, was one of Napoleon's future marshals who refused to support the coup. Nonetheless, he subsequently accepted service under Napoleon.

3. Lindqvist, *Napoleon*, 246–47. The Swedish historian, Herman Lindqvist, relates that when Napoleon started his campaign against Russia in 1812, he was beset by a number of health problems, which significantly affected him as a commander.

4. Following his splendid victory at Auerstädt, Davout became the Prince of Eckmuhl. Murat was made King of Naples but thought he ought to be promoted ruler of Spain. That was impossible because Napoleon had given that kingdom to his older brother, Joseph. Napoleon's younger brother, Jerome, became king of Westphalia. Even Bernadotte was at one time aiming higher than the Swedish crown. He confided to Alexander, at their meeting on Aland in August of 1812, that he had some hopes of replacing Napoleon as ruler of France. In his account of Napoleon's 1812 campaign, Caulaincourt (who himself was the Duke of Vincenza) refers to Marshals Murat, Berthiers, and other commanders not by their military titles but as "King of Naples," "Prince of Neuchatel," etc. Some of them paid a price. In his efforts to remain king of Naples, following Napoleon's defeat at Waterloo, Murat ended up being executed

by the Italian part of the Bourbon family. Like Marshal Ney, Murat was given the privilege of himself giving the order of execution. Ultimately, Napoleon paid the biggest price for so freely handing out these royal positions and titles. Joseph's rule was not accepted by the Spaniards. A civil war resulted beginning in 1808, which offered British forces under Wellington an opportunity to join what became known as the Peninsular War. Following Napoleon's disaster in Russia in 1812, the intensifying Peninsular War contributed greatly to Napoleon's failure to defend his empire against the sixth coalition.

5. Chandler, *The Campaigns of Napoleon*, 830. When Ney reappeared, Napoleon awarded him the title "the bravest of the brave" and subsequently made him Duke of Moscow. Considering that Napoleon commenced the Russian campaign less than five months earlier with five hundred to six hundred thousand men, his excitement at Ney saving nine hundred out of his six thousand rearguard demonstrates the extent of the French disaster during those few months.

6. Chandler, *The Campaigns of Napoleon*, 495–97; Lindqvist, *Napoleon*, 321. Bernadotte's corps at the time was stationed in between Auerstädt and Jena with the ability of reaching either battle within a few hours. He first received an order to move toward the battle at Jena. Later, when Napoleon realized Davout's peril, Bernadotte's order was changed, and he was instead ordered to assist Davout. However, Bernadotte persisted in following the first order at a slow pace and arrived too late to participate at Jena and didn't assist Davout at Auerstädt. At Elba, Napoleon indicated that he had written an order for Bernadotte's court martial but changed his mind and tore up the order. A story suggests that Bernadotte was saved because his wife's sister was married to Napoleon's older brother, Joseph. Napoleon felt strongly about protecting the family and could not make himself issue an order that would result in a member being shot. After Auerstädt, Bernadotte got a chance to repair his reputation by pursuing and defeating the remnants of the Prussian forces, which had retired north along the Elbe River.

7. Napoleon issued a prohibition of any trade with Britain in November 1806 in response to Britain's blockade of trade with France. Napoleon's prohibition, referred to as the Continental System, applied to France, any of its allied nations, and nations more or less controlled by France.

8. Caulaincourt, *With Napoleon in Russia*, 5. In a long private conference with Napoleon in June 1811, Caulaincourt told Napoleon that Tsar Alexander had advised him "If... Napoleon makes war on me, it is possible, even probable that we shall be defeated... But that will not mean that he can dictate a peace... We have plenty of room... which means as the Emperor Napoleon has admitted that we need never accept a dictated peace, whatever reverses we may suffer."

9. Vilna, now part of Lithuania, and Grodno, now part of Belarus, became part of the Russian empire in 1795 as a result of the first division of Poland.

10. Caulaincourt, *With Napoleon in Russia*, 70.

11. Clausewitz, *The Campaign of 1812 in Russia*, 76. Clausewitz disagreed with this assessment, however. He felt Napoleon when he left Vitebsk, instead of going south toward the Dnieper, should have advanced on the road from Vitebsk to Smolensk (remaining on the northern side of the Dnieper.) Clausewitz believed that Barclay and Bagration's armies at that time were too far northwest of Smolensk to escape Napoleon's forces on the main road from Smolensk to Moscow and would have been forced into a major, possibly decisive, battle. He considered Napoleon's move south of the Dnieper one of the major errors in Napoleon's campaign.

12. Clausewitz, *The Campaign of 1812 in Russia*, 76. Clausewitz felt if Napoleon had kept his army north of the Dnieper, Smolensk would have been taken without these costly attacks.

13. Caulaincourt, *With Napoleon in Russia*, 89–90. Napoleon expressed great satisfaction at Kutuzov's appointment, assuming it meant the Russian Army was finally prepared for a decisive battle.

14. Reihn, *1812: Napoleon's Russian Campaign*, 244. In addition to some of the artillery being ineffective, Kutuzov had allocated too few of his forces in Bagration's southern section where the major French attacks took place. As pressure increased against Bagration's positions, Barclay, without awaiting instructions from Kutuzov, arranged for a part of his force to move south to support Bagration.

15. Clausewitz, *The Campaign of 1812 in Russia*, 121–22.

16. Lindqvist, *Napoleon*, 449. It seems fairly clear that Kutuzov, for whatever reason, was not totally motivated in moving the main Russian Army in pursuit of Napoleon's drastically weakened forces. Chandler even speculated that Kutuzov may have preferred to see Napoleon escape (Chandler 1995, 845). In response to the British ambassador's suggestion that he step up the pursuit, Kutuzov reportedly responded that he was disinclined to risk the lives of Russian soldiers, when the Russian winter did such a good job in killing off the Frenchmen.

17. Clausewitz, *The Campaign of 1812 in Russia*, foreword, xv.

18. In early 1812, Prussia was in a very weak position in relation to Napoleon. Following Prussia's defeat in its recent conflict, a strong French force under Marshal Davout was positioned close to Berlin. Napoleon advised King Frederick Wilhelm that his failure to join the intended campaign against Alexander would result in Davout's immediate occupation of Berlin and Frederick's dismissal as King. Metternich, foreign minister of Austria, calculated that joining Napoleon might give Austria significant benefits in case Napoleon won the conflict. If Napoleon lost, Metternich assumed both parties would be sufficiently weakened for Austria to choose whichever approach might seem most advantageous.

19. The young major, Carl von Clausewitz, who eventually became the recognized leader of military theory in his generation, went so far as to leave the Prussian military service and to join that of Russia when Napoleon started his campaign in 1812.

20. Clausewitz, *The Campaign of 1812 in Russia,* 133–36. In December 1812, with French troops still in Russia, Clausewitz

accompanied the Russian General Diebitsch to a meeting with General York, commander of the Prussian troops, part of Napoleon's invasion force in June 1812. Following the meeting, York, without consent from his superiors in Berlin, declared that the Prussian troops were now neutral and would no longer support the French. York risked court martial for his act but was received as a hero on his return to Berlin.

21. Riehn, *1812: Napoleon's Russian Campaign*, 222. Chandler, *The Campaigns of Napoleon*, 804. Napoleon recovered from his weakness in Russia soon after his return to Paris in December 1812. In his victories at Lutzen and Bautzen in May 1813, Napoleon displayed his old mastery. It is reported that Napoleon was explaining details of the Swedish victory in 1632 to his staff when he heard cannon fire and realized that Ney's forces were being attacked. He quickly took the steps needed to deal with the situation. However, his newly recruited army was not an adequate replacement for the troops lost in Russia. In particular, the cavalry was not strong enough to carry out an effective pursuit of the retreating enemy. As a result, the combined Prussian-Russian armies, while defeated at Lutzen, managed to avoid what might have been a catastrophic defeat.

22. Caulaincourt, *With Napoleon in Russia*, 68–70.

23. Caulaincourt, *With Napoleon in Russia*, 87. Caulaincourt noted Napoleon's tendency to be "led on and on despite himself and was forced to cover a dozen leagues when he had intended to make only five."

24. Clausewitz, *The Campaign of 1812 in Russia*, 144–45. While St. Petersburg clearly should have been the target for Napoleon's campaign, Clausewitz suggested that the conquest of Moscow might have given Napoleon victory, provided the Grand Army at that time had been at a strength of at least two hundred thousand. In fact, Napoleon had only ninety thousand men when he entered Moscow.

25. Fuller, *Decisive Battles of the Western World*, 171.

26. Lindqvist, *Napoleon,* 451–52. Chandler, *The Campaigns of Napoleon*, 825.

27. Bengtsson, *Karl XII:s Levnad*, 211–12.
28. Moltusov, *Poltava 1709*, 68.
29. Following von Hindenburg's death in 1934, Hitler terminated the Presidential system and made himself head of state, *Fuehrer* (leader), and awarded himself unlimited powers as such and as chancellor.
30. Hjalmar Schacht had been an influential banker since the early 1920s and served as head of the Central Bank for several years during the Weimar Republic. Because of disagreements with Hitler, he was fired as minister of finance in 1937 and removed as head of the Central Bank shortly before the start of the war in 1939.
31. Some American economists have expressed appreciation of Hitler Germany's success in improving the economy and drastically reducing unemployment during the 1930s (John Kenneth Galbraith, *The Age of Uncertainty*, 1977). Guided by Schacht, Germany implemented something close to a Keynesian approach—government spending for a number of projects, primarily military but some civilian (the autobahn, etc.), combined with control of wages and prices (Ahamed, *The Lords of Finance*, 481). Unemployment in the United States peaked at 24 percent in 1933. It was 17 percent in 1939.
32. Hitler later explained he did not want to join the Austro-Hungarian Army because of its mixture of races.
33. B. H. Liddell Hart, *The German Generals*, 92. Both Germany and the Soviet Union took advantage of the Spanish Civil War to test aircraft and tank designs and other military equipment. General Thoma, Guderian's deputy during Barbarossa, told Liddell Hart that he was in charge of all German troops sent to Spain to support General Franco in 1938. The force included Mark I tanks. Thoma said Soviet forces supporting the opposite side were already in Spain when he arrived. Their tanks were heavier and better armed than the German ones. Thoma said he offered an award for any Russian tank captured, so he could study it. The Russian troops were commanded by Colonel Koniev, a future marshal of the Soviet Union. No group of tanks

from Britain or France were tested in the Spanish Civil War. For Germany this war was a valuable opportunity for improving its Air Force.

34. De Gaulle, *The Complete War Memoirs*, 37–43. Renault, prime minister during the German invasion in the spring of 1940, had read de Gaulle's book and had been impressed. He offered de Gaulle the opportunity to command one of France's few armored divisions. De Gaulle promptly executed his theories in counterattacks, which drove back the German forces. Following this success, de Gaulle was promoted to Brigadier General and appointed deputy secretary of defense.

35. Heinz Guderian, *Achtung—Panzer!* (Stuttgart, 1939).

36. General Thoma told Liddell Hart that the French tanks were in some respects better than the best of the German ones but too slow and ineffectually employed (B. H. Liddell Hart, *The German Generals*, 94). De Gaulle believed if the French mechanized forces, including some three thousand tanks, had been organized in functioning groups, the Germans could have faced stiff resistance. De Gaulle, *The Complete War Memoirs*, 36.

37. Tukhachevsky was well familiar with the theories of Liddell Hart, Fuller and Guderian, and Tukhachevsky's theory for the use of mechanized forces was quite similar to theirs.

38. In connection with the prosecution of Tukhachevsky, the Germans provided aid to the prosecutors. Heinrich Himmler, head of the Gestapo and his close assistant, Reinhard Heydrich, prepared fake material that was leaked to Soviet authorities and supported the case against Tukhachevsky.

39. The purges eliminated three of five marshals, thirteen of fifteen Army commanders, and 154 of 186 division commanders.

40. Tukhachevsky and a number of other executed high Soviet officers were declared innocent in 1957 during Khrushchev's reign as chairman of the Politburo.

41. The British and the French also started rearming in 1934 following Hitler's repudiation of the Versailles Treaty. The British made some important improvements in fighter airplanes (Hawker Hurricane and Supermarine Spitfire), which became

crucial in the Battle for Britain in 1940. Overall, however, the British-French preparations fell far short of what was done in Germany.

42. "Stalin first combined with Zinoviev and Kamenev to weaken Trotsky's political position. Within three years he formed a coalition with the other major group (headed by Bukharin) to destroy the political power of Zinoviev, Kamenev, and Trotsky. Within another two years (1929) Stalin 'redirected his fire' at the Bukharin group and at the Sixteenth Party Congress (1930) arranged the political *liquidation* of Bukharin and other opposition leaders (Rykov, Tomskii, and others)." V. Rapoport, by V. Treml.

43. Some of them, like Voroshilov and Budyonny, were old cronies from the civil war.

44. B. H. Liddell Hart, *History*, 146.

45. In December 1940, Soviet Foreign Minister Vyacheslav Molotov visited Berlin to explore with Joachim von Ribbentrop, his German counterpart, and other German officials the possibility of the Soviet Union joining the Axis Pact between Germany, Italy, and Japan. No decision was made. Molotov left and was supposed to study the matter further and continue discussions at a later date. However, these discussions did not affect Hitler's determination to attack the Soviet Union.

46. Hjalmar Schacht, president of the German Central bank at the time, was another prominent participant in this conspiracy.

47. B. H. Liddell Hart, *The German Generals*, 174. Some of the German generals questioned the assumption that the Russian troops would not retreat deep into Russia as they had done in 1812. They had doubts as to how the German Army would be able to deal with such a situation. Hitler reassured them by claiming that he had information indicating that Stalin would be overthrown as soon as his forces had suffered a few setbacks.

48. Frederick I, Barbarossa, was crowned emperor of the Holy Roman Empire by Pope Adrian IV in 1155. Most of what today is Germany was part of the Holy Roman Empire at the time.

Barbarossa has been considered one of the Empire's strongest rulers.

49. In January 1941, Pavlov had been featured speaker in a conference Stalin had arranged to provide more information about armored warfare. He was recalled to Moscow by Stalin within days of the Minsk defeat and was executed for incompetence.

50. Stahel, *Operation Barbarossa,* 315–18.

51. Hitler's unbounded optimism concerning the success of Barbarossa had made him uninterested in the possibility of Japanese participation at the time Barbarossa was launched. However, as the operations in Russia were getting increasingly difficult in the end of July 1941, Hitler changed his mind and suggested to the Japanese ambassador in Berlin that destroying Russia ought to be a principal objective of both countries. With a Japanese Army of seven hundred thousand stationed close to the Soviet border, the Japanese Army leadership favored action. However, the Japanese prime minister and the leaders of the Japanese Navy and Air Force disagreed. They felt Southeast Asia was the priority, in particular as German victory in the east no longer looked so easy.

52. B. H. Liddell Hart, *The German Generals,* 185.

53. The Japanese decision in July to stay out of the conflict eliminated a potential problem for Zhukov in bringing critically needed reserves from the Far East.

54. Churchill, vol. 4, 125. Concerning the German submarine warfare, Churchill commented in his memoirs: "It would have been wise of the Germans to stake all upon it."

55. Stahel, *Operation Barbarossa,* 437–38.

56. Churchill, vol. 4, 327.

57. B. H. Liddell Hart, *History,* 488. Stalin did allow Molotov to meet for peace talks with von Ribbentrop in Kirovograd in the Ukraine in June 1943. At that time, following the Stalingrad victory, the Soviet was in a far stronger position than in the spring of 1942.

58. Churchill, vol. 4, 322. Churchill worried about Soviet-German peace negotiations.

59. Hitler's assurance to von Kleist that allied troops would protect his exposed flanks contrasted with Hitler's rejection of use of Hungarian troops in June 1941, following a suggestion to that effect by von Rundstedt. Hitler then had declared that only German troops were good enough to be part of Barbarossa.

60. Churchill, vol. 4, 495.

61. Stalin put tremendous pressure on the civilian population to take part in the battle. Stalin dealt harshly with deserters and people suspected of desertion or not putting up enough of a fight. The number of people executed for these crimes has been reported as running in the thousands. Nonetheless, there were regiments fighting on the German side, which included large number of Russians. Nikita Khrushchev served as a political commissar in Stalingrad during the battle.

62. The German Air Force detachment, supporting the Sixth Army in Stalingrad, was commanded by General Wolfram von Richthofen, a cousin of Manfred von Richthofen, the Red Baron, the most successful German fighter pilot in World War I. Wolfram got his introduction to air combat flying in his cousin's wing in 1918 in what turned out to be the Red Baron's last flight.

63. Rokossovsky found out that the NKVD relied for his prosecution on the claimed testimony of an officer he had known in the Civil War. Rokossovsky also knew that this individual had died in that war. So at his final court hearing, he told the court he would sign a confession if the NKVD produced his accuser. He was found innocent but was still kept in jail for another two years.

64. It has also been suggested that he believed a German victory at Kursk might make Stalin inclined to discuss peace, in view of his frustration with the continuing delay of a second front in France.

65. B. H. Liddell Hart, *History*, 488. It seems the Germans missed a chance to get out of a losing campaign by asking for too much. One would assume that if future prospects were even between parties in a war, a return to the situation at the start of hostili-

ties would be a logical peace proposal. By June 1943, the prospects of the Soviet Union were clearly better than those of the Germans and the situation for the Germans was steadily deteriorating. Nonetheless, Von Ribbentrop's proposal suggested that the Germans were winning.

66. Guderian, now in charge of developing new mobile forces, objected to a new offensive anywhere on the eastern front. He thought it would just waste German troops and equipment, in particular tanks. He tried to convince Hitler but failed.

67. Hughes and Mann, *Inside Hitler's Germany*, 145–46. The Panther and Tiger tanks were very good, possibly superior to any enemy tank. However, the German industry was unable to produce them in sufficient numbers. From their introduction in 1943 until the end of the war only five thousand Panthers and one thousand Tigers were manufactured. In comparison, it has been estimated that at least fifty-five thousand T-34s and a similar number of Sherman tanks were produced during World War II. Although the T-34 production covered a fifty percent longer period than Germany's production of Panthers and Tigers, the discrepancy in numbers nonetheless demonstrate the rather hopeless positions of the Germans the longer the war went on. According to some historians, the German failure to adopt the mass production system used in the United States, Britain, and even the Soviet Union contributed to the German inability to match the production levels of its enemies when it came to tanks, airplanes, and other war equipment.

68. The Soviet Army had received numerous new tanks produced in the factories in the Ural mountains. These tanks were mostly the very effective T-34 but also some heavier tanks. Some tanks had also been provided by the United States and Britain.

69. Stahel, *Operation Barbarossa*, 44–45, 315.

70. Stahel, *Operation Barbarossa*, 226–27, 331.

71. Stahel, *Operation Barbarossa*, 281.

72. Stahel, *Operation Barbarossa*, 344–45. Although an Air Force general, in November 1941 Kesselring was put in charge of

all German forces in the Mediterranean. He led the German troops in Italy in 1943–44.

73. B. H. Liddell Hart, *The German Generals*, 199. There were some indications that in planning the Caucasus offensive, Hitler and some of his planners were considering a follow-up move from Stalingrad north toward Moscow. Apparently, Halder was able to convince Hitler that such plans went far beyond the capability of the available forces.

74. Stahel, *Operation Barbarossa*, 276. Hitler considered Halder to be a mediocre bureaucrat.

75. Gunther points out how Hitler avoided a number of traps, including tempting opportunities to grab power without waiting for political developments, during his gradual ascendancy. Once chancellor, he deftly handled one challenge after another, violating treaties, invading foreign countries, and issuing threats of invasion without incurring any significant negative reaction from the two countries primarily charged with the responsibility of maintaining peace, stability, and the Versailles treaty in Europe.

76. Olson, *Citizens of London,* 140–41. During his visit home from his work in London in November 1941, journalist Edward R. Murrow expressed his intense disappointment with the American public's disinterest in the war in Europe and the strength of isolationists like Charles Lindbergh and Senator Burton Wheeler.

77. According to Guderian's principles for mobile warfare adopted by the German military, surprise was needed for attacks to succeed.

78. B. H. Liddell Hart, *The German Generals*, 110–11.

79. Some of Stalin's purges were actually continued following the start of Barbarossa.

80. Even Marshal Rokossovsky, who himself had barely survived Stalin's purges, at one time called for the execution of some Russian commanders for incompetence.

81. Lindqvist, *Napoleon,* 450.

82. Voltaire, *The History of Charles XII*, 154. Following the Russian victory at Poltava, Peter arranged a celebration dinner at which Field Marshal Rehnskjold, top commander of the defeated Swedish army, was placed in the seat of honor next to Peter. According to Voltaire, Peter then called for a toast for the captured Swedish officers who had taught the Russians how to win. Massie, *Peter the Great*, 523. Peter also made generous offers to Swedish officers he thought could be of use.

83. Napoleon's rather arrogant decision to install his brother Joseph as king of Spain was a major cause of the war. Spain, a former ally, became an enemy. The development provided the British an opportunity to bring troops into Portugal and Spain to support local forces in their battle against the French. It might be argued that Napoleon could not afford to engage in a huge Russian campaign before the Peninsula War was settled. Wellington's victory at Vittoria in Spain on June 20, 1813, contributed greatly to the Prussian-Russian coalition regaining strength following its defeat at Lutzen and Bautzen and to persuade Austria to join the new alliance.

84. Hitler's failure was not his absence from the front lines; presence there cannot be expected by the supreme commander in modern warfare. The problem was his micromanagement from far behind the scene.

85. Stahel, *Operation Barbarossa*, 78–89. This decision was based on insufficient and inaccurate information. During the planning process for Barbarossa, Halder, von Paulus, and other top commanders, anxious to provide Hitler the information he wanted, sometimes withheld or distorted information unfavorable to the German plans.

86. From his conversations with Alexander, Caulaincourt knew that it was highly unlikely that Alexander and his military commanders would allow the Russian forces to be dragged into a battle that would give Napoleon a chance of a quick victory. That is probably why Caulaincourt tried hard to dissuade Napoleon from attacking Russia. Unfortunately for France, Napoleon was not convinced by Caulaincourt's arguments.

SOURCES

Ahamed, Liaquat. *The Lords of Finance: The Bankers Who Broke the World*. London: Penguin Books, 2009.

Bengtsson, Frans G. *Karl XII:s Levnad*. Stockholm, Sweden: Nordstedt,1936.

Caulaincourt, Armand de, and Duke de Vicenza. *With Napoleon in Russia*. New York: William Morrow & Co., 1935.

Chandler, David G., *The Campaigns of Napoleon*. London: Weidenfeld & Nicholson, 1995.

Clausewitz, Carl von. *The Campaign of 1812 in Russia*. Cambridge, MA: Blue Crane Books, 1996.

Churchill, Winston. *The Second World War*, Volume 4; *The Hinge of Fate*. Boston: Houghton Mifflin Company, 1950.

Fuller, J. F. C. *Decisive Battles of the Western World*, Volume II. London: Cassel & Co., 1955.

Gaulle, Charles de. *The Complete War Memoirs*. New York: Carroll & Graf Publishers, 1998.

Gunther, John. *Inside Europe*. Amazon, 1938.

Hart, B. H. Liddell. *The German Generals Talk*. New York: Quill, 1979.

Hart, B. H. Liddell. *History of the Second World War*. Old Saybrook, CT: Konecky & Konecky, 1970.

Hughes, Matthew, and Chris Mann. *Inside Hitler's Germany*. New York: MUF Books, 2000.

Lindqvist, Herman. *Napoleon*. Stockholm, Sweden: Nordstedts, 2003.

Lyth, Einar, and P. Konovaltjuk. *The Way to Poltava, the Battle of Lesnaya*. Svenskt Militarhistoriskt Bibliotek, 2010.

Massie, Robert K. *Peter the Great*. New York, 1980.

Moltusov, V. A. *Poltava 1709*. Vandpunkten, Svenskt Militarhistoriskt Bibliotek, 2010.

Olson, Lynne. *Citizens of London*. New York: Random House, 2010.

Riehn, Richard K. *1812: Napoleon's Russian Campaign*. New York: John Wiley & Sons, Inc., 1991.

Stahel, David. *Operation Barbarossa and Germany's Defeat in the East*. New York: Cambridge University Press, 2010.

Voltaire, Francois-Marie K. de. *The History of Charles XII, King of Sweden*. Barnes & Noble Books, 1933.

ABOUT THE AUTHOR

Adolf Af Jochnick is an American with dual American-Swedish citizenship. He grew up in Sweden during the Second World War, which stimulated an early interest in military history. He subsequently studied this subject while in the Swedish military, in which he has held a commission as an officer, and at the University of Stockholm. In 1958 he graduated from the Harvard Law School and has practiced law for most of his career. In 2014, he completed a book about the battles between Russia, Sweden, and the Ottoman Empire in the early eighteenth century. He lives in Cambridge, Massachusetts, with his wife Liz.

CPSIA information can be obtained
at www.ICGtesting.com
Printed in the USA
BVOW11s2037070617
486298BV00014BA/36/P